MY HERO

JULIE CAPULET

Caleb McCabe just returned from a tour of duty. He's shell-shocked. Loud noises make him jump. He feels like an outcast in civilian society. When Caleb meets a gorgeous, fun-loving redhead named Violet, he knows he can't handle a relationship, especially with a dream girl like her. But that doesn't stop him from thinking about her day and night.

Violet Jameson is studying for a degree in psychology. When she meets the ultra-hot combat hero Caleb, she's riveted not only by his rugged good looks but also by his obvious vulnerabilities. She yearns to get close to him, and to begin to heal him. They share a night of passion that's so hot she realizes she's not only in lust but in love.

For Violet's sake, Caleb tries to stay away. He wants her more than he can bear, but he's afraid of hurting her with his own emotional scars. The problem is, no matter how much he fights his obsession, he can't stop himself. He has to make her his. He knows in his heart she's the one.

Caleb and Violet are meant for each other, but will his dark damages get in the way of their Happily Ever After?

My Hero is a sexy standalone novella starring a battle-scarred alpha hero and the sweet, sassy redhead who changes everything.

McCabe Brothers Series

JULIE CAPULET ROMANCE

MY HERO

Copyright © 2020, 2024 Julie Capulet

ASIN: B083Y3VKBW

ISBN-13: 979-8638811501

MY HERO is a work of fiction. While reference may be made to actual historical events or existing locations, the names, characters, places and incidents portrayed in this book are fictitious. Any resemblance to actual persons, living or dead, events, business establishments or locales is entirely coincidental.

Cover photography: Rafa G. Catala

www.juliecapulet.com

Dedicated all those suffering who stay strong and bear the unbearable. And to those who sometimes break down. And to my brother, who deployed three times.

Note to readers:

This book deals with the subject of Post Traumatic Stress Disorder and also references suicide (off-page and in the past).

It also has a sweet, hot, romantic HEA.

My
HERO

1

Violet

"TODAY'S TOPIC IS ..." My psychology professor starts writing some words on the whiteboard. " ... Post Traumatic Stress Disorder, which is, as suggested, triggered by a life event that has in some way been traumatic. Today we'll talk about the causes that can lead to PTSD."

I'm riveted, as usual. I wish I could say there are days that Professor Jackson's lectures are boring, when I find myself staring out the window while I daydream about football players, like a normal person would. This isn't quite the case (okay, sometimes I daydream about football players).

In every other area of my life, I'm an outgoing, fun-loving party girl. But when it comes to the study of psychology, I'm a total nerd. I've known I wanted to be a shrink since I was around seven years old, which is probably pretty weird. Who knows they want to be a psychoanalyst when they're seven years old?

Me, as it turns out.

I have three older brothers. I used to use them as my patients, which they of course hated. But there was no escaping me. I made them lie on the couch while I worked through my list of questions, solving all their problems. To this day, they refuse to sit on a couch in the same room as me. But all three of them are well-adjusted, mostly-happy, highly-paid professionals with degrees and nice girlfriends, so I like to think I had something to do with all that.

Now, I'm a freshman studying—you guessed it— psychology. I'm only about a month in, and I'm already loving it. My plan is to be a licensed psychotherapist by the time I'm twenty-seven. A weird aspiration, possibly, but that's just me. Along the way, though, I also plan on having a fabulous time. Also me. I'm one of those people that can't *not* have a good time. Some people call me "bubbly," "extro-verted," "a social butterfly," etc. I like to have fun. I figure that's not a bad thing, so I just go with it.

Professor Jackson continues. "People with PTSD may experience a variety of symptoms including … " More writing on the white board. "Violet, would you please read out this list?" Professor Jackson loves my enthusiasm.

So I read out the list.

- 1) Feeling emotionally numb
- 2) Feeling detached from family and friends

- 3) Having difficulty maintaining close relationships
- 4) Lacking interest in activities they once enjoyed

"Thank you, Violet," says Professor Jackson. "Class, your homework for Monday is to read pages 223 to 405, which cover these and other symptoms."

I've already read the textbook, and I've already read widely about PTSD, in detail. It must be a terrible thing to go through and it makes me feel grateful.

I'm lucky.

My life has been outrageously trauma-free so far. (Except for one thing, which I prefer not to dwell on.) My parents are happily married and still live in our family home back in Wilmington. My three brothers are rowdy, fun, awesome people. They're basically my own personal body-guards, support network and best friends. When my phone buzzes in my pocket, it's usually one of them, checking up on me, like they do on practically an hourly basis.

My phone buzzes in my pocket.

Will it be Liam, Henry or Aiden this time?

Come over to Bo's after your class and hang out with me.

Not my brothers. It's a snap from my new roommate, Millie. Things have been a little crazy for her lately because she just so happens to have hooked up with the star freaking quarterback and is now practically living with him.

Once they got started, it became *very* intense *very* quickly, which is why it's been so crazy.

I convinced her to come with me to the first game of the season, on our very first day at school. There we were, innocently watching the game, getting to know each other, minding our own business ... and that's when it happened. The über-hot quarterback glanced up at the Jumbotron, which was, in that moment, zeroed in on Millie. She's gorgeous but sort of tries to hide it because she's shy AF. But the cameraperson just stayed on her as a gust of wind blew her hat off, letting loose her hair, which is a really unusual and amazing shade of pale reddish-blond. I don't know why she keeps it hidden all the time, but she always wears it tucked into her hat. And suddenly there it was in all its golden glory, dramatic and glowing under the spotlights on the big screen. The quarterback froze in place like he was starstruck, for so long that everyone in the stands also turned to look at what *he* was looking at. And then it became this *event* because everyone was wondering who this beautiful, mysterious girl was that had brought the quarterback and the entire game to a standstill. By then, the coach was going ballistic and Bo almost got taken off because he was so distracted. But he managed to get it together and they won the game. Which we missed the end of, because Millie was mortified and insisted on leaving. Everyone was staring at her and she hates that kind of attention, so I went back to the dorm with her to make sure she was okay.

But then, within less than an hour, the whole thing went viral. One of Bo's friends, another football player, had posted something about how Bo was looking for Millie. By then she'd been dubbed "the Jumbotron Angel" and it was all #BoWantsToKnow and so on.

Long story short, with the help of basically the entire campus, Bo's team ended up tracking her down. It took him a while to find her, but once he did, they went from zero to sixty pretty fast.

They're perfect for each other, you can just tell. I'm not an expert at matchmaking or anything, but it's just a fact. You can see it by the way they gaze at each other in this annoyingly (in a good way and basically in the kind of way you wish *you* were gazing at someone) loved-up kind of way.

Anyway, I haven't seen a lot of Millie since all that happened. Most likely, she's in Bo's to-die-for mansion.

Even though Millie and I haven't known each other that long, and she never even ended up spending a single night in our dorm room, we really clicked, and I miss her.

A lot of people would be happy to have their own room. I just don't happen to be one of them. Growing up as the youngest of four (actually five, but that's a story for another day), we always had a lot of people coming and going in our house. My parents are both social people and my brothers always had a lot of girls chasing after them, coming around and hanging out. And my mom likes to cook so is always putting on little impromptu parties for everyone that comes over. And my brothers are big and loud and have a lot of stuff everywhere, so there's always a lot of people and activity and fun, which I thrive on.

Sitting in my empty dorm room all alone sucks. I don't

really want to go back there after class to stare at the four walls. I've already done my homework, because, as mentioned, I'm obsessed and have already read my psych textbooks from cover to cover.

So when I see Millie's snap of her sitting in a hot tub— *Bo has practice so I'm all alone. I need you!*—my afternoon plans slide into place. Bo's house is incredible. His parents died a few years ago, I'm not sure how. Millie said Bo has two older brothers. One is a CEO of his own company and the other one is in the military. He's been in Afghanistan for a year, she said.

Shit, is what I was thinking.

I really can't imagine going to war. I admire the hell out of those people, putting themselves on the line like that.

Professor Jackson is still talking. "Most people who go through these traumatic events have difficulty adjusting to normal life. They might have trouble talking to people in normal social situations. They often have a hard time adjusting and coping. If left untreated, their symptoms can last for years, or even a lifetime. But with good care and good self-care, they *can* get better, often much better."

Another snap from Millie. *When are you coming?!?*

I message her back. *My class finishes in ten. I'll be right over.*

2

CALEB

"McCABE! You've been given a direct order! Leave him! Return to your post immediately. There's nothing more you can do here! This soldier is dead. Let the medics take him."

It can't be true. My three closest friends in this hell have all been killed within the past three days. They call me one of the best snipers we have, but it makes no difference. I pick them off, but it makes no difference. I follow orders, but it makes no difference. My men get shot anyway. Their brains splatter against dusty, shell-pocked walls and their blood spills onto the ground like thick dark-red oil. It's all over me. And then I realize it's not Logan's blood that's all over me. It's mine.

I'm glad.

I want it to be mine. I want to trade my blood for Logan's. I want to rewind time and take his bullet. I want his blood to ooze back into him, so he wakes up and cracks another joke. Why should I live if he can't?

My pain feels good. So fucking deserved. And when oblivion over-takes me, it's the most peaceful feeling I've had in an entire goddamn year.

"Excuse me, mister?" Someone's tapping me on the shoulder. "Mister?"

I jerk awake and some kid is staring at me over the seats of the bus. My hands feel empty and I realize it's because I'm not clutching my rifle.

It takes me a second to get my bearings. I'm on a bus. I'm on my way home. I've been discharged. I'm mostly recovered. I spent the last month in a military hospital. Now I'm back on American soil. I'm alive and I'm not holding an M4 carbine.

"I think you were having a nightmare," says the kid.

I don't respond. I just turn away from him and look out the window.

Thankfully, he goes away, putting his earbuds back in and scrolling on his phone. Thank fuck. I'm hardly going to explain to some clueless kid about my "nightmare." My whole fucking *life* is a nightmare. I can't get away from it. It fills my dreams and every waking second. It's all I can think about. It consumes me, like I'm being eaten alive by my gruesomely-detailed memories.

The landscape looks the same. Vast. Greener than the desert. More neon and plastic and brick. More slow-paced normality, if there is such a thing. We pull into the bus station and I pick up my duffle bag. I grab a taxi and give the driver the address. The last thing I feel like doing is talking, so I don't, even though the taxi driver rambles on about something I don't care about. I can hardly bear the familiarity of my neighborhood as we drive through it. Everything is the same—yet nothing will ever be the same. How can it be? The contradictions hurt my head and my heart so deeply, for a second I'm wondering if I'm having a heart attack.

Unfortunately, I'm not.

We pull up in front of my gate and I pay the guy. He thanks me gushingly and I realize I've given him a two hundred percent tip. He looks so happy, I tell him to keep it, and I wonder if I'll ever feel that emotion again. *Happy.* The word itself annoys me. None of *them* will ever feel happy again. And neither will I.

I remember the code for the gate, even though it's not something I've thought about for a year. I walk up the driveway. It looks nice. It's a beautiful place, I can vaguely recognize.

The front door of my house is unlocked, which is good, since I don't have a key. Gage emailed, saying he'll be in town as soon as he can. He's got a company takeover or something but says he wants to see me. Bo will be around but is probably at practice. I remember how intense the coaches work you. I used to be on the team. An all-star, not that it matters at this point. My injuries mean that I'll never play ball again, not that I would want to at this point.

All that feels like a long time ago.

An easier time, before daggers of sorrow became everything.

I hear voices coming from the pool area.

Girls' voices.

I drop my duffle bag and step through the door, wondering if Bo is with them.

Two girls in bikinis are lying on loungers.

They both stare at me and I stare back.

My brain can't quite handle this. I haven't seen a girl in a bikini—or any woman for that matter who isn't a war-hardened soldier in combat fatigues—for a very long time. They're both gorgeous, especially the one with the long, copper-bright hair and the white bikini, the curvier one, the one who's smiling and was laughing until I stepped into view. The other girl, who has very pale red-blond hair, says, "You must be Caleb. Hi, I'm Millie. This is Violet."

It's strange to hear my name. No one's called me anything but McCabe since I left for Afghanistan.

"Oh. Bo's brother," says the redhead. "The soldier." She stands up and starts walking over to me. She has bright green eyes and a sprinkling of golden freckles across her nose. Her face reminds me of that word again: *happy*. In fact I don't think I've ever seen a person who sort of *radiates* happiness as much as this girl does. My eyes want to drink in all that golden skin and the long legs and mind-numbing curves, barely covered at all by those tiny shreds of wet white fabric. That dazzling, welcoming, delighted smile.

But I can't even look. This is *way* too much.

I can't handle it. If she touches me, I might fucking self-combust. Every nerve ending in my body is crackling, like I'm about to get a severe, hot electric shock that could very possibly jolt me over the edge of sanity.

I take a step back.

Her smile falters a little as she notices my reaction. But she holds her ground. She's not intimidated like the other girl seems to be, who's also standing up now but keeping her distance. I probably weigh as much as both of them, plus one, put together. All we do in our downtime is sleep, train and work out and I'm basically a hard, ruthless fighting machine at this point.

"Hi, Caleb," says the dazzling girl, and I see now that her hair is a bright shade of red but also has all these other shades of gold and deeper reds and strawberry blond in it too, like she's been painted all the colors of the sun. Her green eyes have shards of lighter, off-neon green and gold in them, as though she's plugged in. Her lips are a heart-breaking shade of pink. She's just so freakishly ... *colorful,* in every possible way. I have the urge to shade my eyes from her. "It must feel strange to get home after being away for so long." She's talking to me carefully. Her voice is almost soothing—if I were capable of being soothed.

The problem is, I'm not.

The only thing I'm capable of being is one hundred percent fucked up.

So I take another step back. I don't even reply to her. I can't bring myself to say anything at all.

I return to the coolness of the house, relieved to be away from all that … *glory.* That smile and all that bouncy softness and warm skin and, basically, way the fuck too much of everything. Details that belong to a place I'm a long way away from. Heaven, maybe. Heaven on earth.

I walk to the fridge and drink all the orange juice straight out of the container. Then I go upstairs to my old room, which—incredibly—is entirely unchanged. I strip down to my boxers, throw my fatigues over a chair, and reach to pull the curtains closed. I need some sweet relief from the overly sunny daylight. Before I can fully close the curtains, though, I notice the two girls are getting into the redhead's car. My movement catches her eye and she looks up.

She looks so healthy and perfect and beautiful in her tight jeans and her pink sweater that I feel like I'm having another one of those heart attacks. She's a goddess. A pure, undamaged dream. There's no way in hell I would ever inflict her with my own scars or dirty her with the fucked-up mess I've become. I wouldn't even consider it.

I don't know if there's any hope for me at this point. I'm too far gone.

I pull the curtains closed, blocking her from view. Then I crawl into bed, where I plan to stay for a long time. I feel like I haven't slept—really slept—in years.

Even so, my mind retraces the colors of her hair, the golden smoothness of her skin, sparkling with drops of glinting water. The taut little peaks of her nipples under that ridiculously-skimpy bikini.

How easy it would have been to rip off those tiny shreds of fabric … with hardly any effort at all.

The car starts up loudly, startling me, the noise reminding me of diesel fumes and the smell of gunpowder. Dust. Pain. Blood.

Every memory and every detail cuts deeper into my regret. I gave it every fucking thing I had, and I still couldn't save them.

Much later, somehow, I fall into the blissful darkness of sleep. All I really want to do is stay there.

3

Violet

ONCE MY CLASS FINISHES, I pick up a pizza and drive over to Bo's mansion. I've been here before, a few times, with Millie. She lets me in and gives me a huge hug. She's in her bikini with a towel wrapped around her. "I'm so glad you're here, roomie."

"Me too. The dorm is boring without you. What time will Bo be back?"

"Around six, he said."

We go into the pool area, which has a pool and a hot tub, and folding doors that lead to an outdoor kitchen and dining area, fire pit and sitting area looking out over the lake. In other words, everything you could ever dream of. This place is ridiculous.

Millie told me the McCabe brothers' father ran a successful investment company, and their mother was a clothing designer, but that both of them died a few years ago.

So, even though the house is beautiful, it feels a little sad. I think about my own house, which is nowhere near as big as this one, with its bustle and activity and laughter. There, it always feels too cluttered and crowded and disorganized, but always *inviting*. Homey and warm. This house feels too big, too grand and too quiet.

But we make the most of it, like I always do. We swim. I splash her and she laughs and splashes me back. Then we sit in the hot tub for a while, enjoying the killer view out over the fields and a picturesque lake with a dock house. We eat pizza and drink iced tea and sit in the sunny alcove with the loungers, just talking about random stuff, like you do with your new best friend.

Millie and I have bonded pretty quickly over the past month. Maybe it's the newness of college and the intensity of everything that happens when you first leave home. She never had much of a home life. She doesn't really like to talk about it, but she mentioned that she never had a father and her mother was an addict who died of an overdose. I don't push her to go into details. It's obviously something that might make a person feel guarded and self-conscious.

Little by little, though, she's learning to trust me. That's what I *do*, after all. I listen. I gently coax out the painful stuff so it can be worked through and dealt with. It's what I'm planning on making my career out of, so I think each question through. I take care not to push too hard or dig deeper than she's ready for. "You okay with everything that's happening?" She told me she never even had a boyfriend before Bo. "How are things going?"

She smiles, but there's more to it than just blind contentedness. "*Intense*. To put it mildly."

"Like ... good intense?"

She twirls an end strand of her hair. "Amazing. Except I sometimes wonder if we're taking things *way* too fast. We're already living together and I've only known him for a month. And when we're alone together, he ..." Millie pauses.

It's not hard to guess what she was going to say. "... wants to have sex 24/7? I think that's pretty obvious by the way he looks at you, sweetie."

She blushes. Then she laughs. "I guess so."

"He might be making up for lost time." It had been all over the internet, that Bo McCabe, the hunky, scorching-hot starting quarterback, had been saving himself for "the real thing." Which was why it went viral when he chased after Millie. And why it continues to go viral because he barely lets her out of his sight except when he's playing football.

The two of them have been inseparable. And the whole story has made Bo even more bankable, especially since his team has won every game so far this season. They're calling Millie his lucky charm.

"Bo said his brother Caleb is coming home soon," she tells me. "The one who's been in Afghanistan. Some shrapnel from an explosion hit him and injured him pretty badly. Some of the other guys in his regiment were *killed*, Bo said."

"Oh my god."

"Yeah. But Bo said Caleb should make a full recovery."

Physically, at least, I can't help thinking. I've been reading about this exact topic. Emotionally, things like that can stay with you for a long time.

"He's coming home to rest and recuperate," she says. "I think I'll move back into the dorm when he gets here. Bo wants me to stay, but Caleb most likely just wants to hang out with his brother and have some peace and quiet."

Millie is the quietest person I've ever met. "I'm sure he wouldn't mind having you here. This place is huge and you're hardly loud. Not like me, for example. When's he coming home?"

"Bo isn't sure. It could be any day."

"Well, I hope you *do* move back to the dorm. If I have to spend another second alone in that room I might implode from sheer boredom."

Before she can reply, someone steps into the pool area. A very *big* someone. It's startling, that we didn't even hear him coming.

At first I think it's Bo. But pretty quickly I realize it's definitely not Bo. He looks a lot like Bo but he's even taller and burlier—which is saying something. He's dressed in army clothes and his dark hair is cut in the military style but has grown out a little, like he's overdue for his regulation haircut.

And if I thought Bo McCabe was gorgeous, *this* McCabe takes the meaning of the word to a whole new freaking level.

He's muscular as fuck. He has dark blue eyes that could almost be described as violet (my favorite color, for obvious reasons), and thick black lashes. The color of his eyes is striking. The haunted look *behind* his eyes is even more striking. I've just met the hottest guy I've ever seen in my life, but he's got some serious layers going on. He's spooked-looking and stormy. Like a hurricane of emotion and issues and all kinds of crazy baggage just stepped into the room and stirred up the vibe. I can feel his effect squalling around me in a way that's almost unsettling, because it seems bigger than this moment. His storm isn't something I'm going to forget or recover from in a hurry, I can just tell. His outrageous energy isn't just chaotic and feverish and turbulent, it's ... magnetic.

Wow.

I guess it isn't entirely surprising that his eyes are wild. He just returned from a year of combat and a month-long stint in the hospital recovering from being shot by ISIS or some freaking thing.

"You must be Caleb," says Millie. "Hi, I'm Millie. This is Violet."

He doesn't say anything. He just stands there, staring at us, like he's still shell-shocked. Or newly shell-shocked.

"Oh. Bo's brother," I say, even though we'd just been talking about him and it obviously *is* Caleb. "The soldier."

I stand up slowly and walk over to him, partly because he looks so stunned. I almost have the urge to give him a hug (which is clearly not a good idea). It's sort of fascinating to watch the range of emotions flicker across his expression.

This is my thing, of course: watching expressions, reading body language—*and what a body!* is what I'm also thinking. I can't help myself. He's *unbelievably* buff.

Whatever emotions Caleb McCabe is dealing with are, very obviously, a lot heavier than anything I've dealt with before. Not that I've dealt with all that much, since the only people I've ever (amateurishly, it has to be said) diagnosed are my brothers.

But there's actually more to the story of my brothers than I've mentioned. All that stuff about how I'm bubbly and outgoing and how I like to have fun—it's all true. But it's not *only* because that's my personality. The reason I wanted to be a shrink in the first place isn't *just* because it occurred to me one day out of the blue.

My oldest brother Joe committed suicide when I was seven years old.

He was the oldest son, a football star, a straight-A student, popular, a shining gem of a human being. Possibly my parents' favorite, though none of us could blame them for that. Joe was *everyone's* favorite. He was kind and charming and funny and beautiful and smart. He had a lot of friends and girls chasing after him everywhere he went. Everyone loved him. His life was charmed. Things he touched tended to turn to gold.

There was simply no reason for him to do what he did.

He did it anyway. And we never quite knew why.

There'd been no note, no clues, no signs. At least not to me. Even though I was very young, I'd always been sensitive to people's emotions. Joe used to call me his "little empath." I never really understood what that meant until later, which only made it hurt even more.

I'd taken my brother's suicide personally.

How could he leave us like that? How could he do that to me? *His only sister, who loved him most of all? Why hadn't he let me listen to his fears and his reasons? He would have known how much it would hurt me. Why hadn't he let me at least* try *to save him?*

From then on, all I ever wanted to do was fix people, by guiding them out of the places that hurt, so they could find it in themselves to keep going. That's why I'd psychoanalyzed my other brothers until they couldn't take it anymore. I wanted to help them heal. Maybe they let me do it because they'd recognized that, at the same time, they were helping *me* heal too.

We kept going.

We laughed *more*, even if we were also crying more. We lived each day like we were living for us and for Joe, pouring as much enthusiasm and fun into everything we did. Almost like we were trying to pack two lives into each one of ours.

I've never told anyone who didn't already know about Joe's suicide, and I haven't told Millie. We're getting to the point where I could confide in her about something like that, but the right moment hasn't really come up yet. So I just keep it close to my heart and when people tell me I'm bubbly and fun-loving, I agree, because I am, mostly.

I don't know what it is about Caleb McCabe that makes me think of Joe, but something does.

"Hi, Caleb," I say softly.

Caleb doesn't say a word. He seems stunned by our presence here. As I walk toward him, he takes a step back.

He stares at me, not blankly, but with that outrageous cocktail of emotion behind his eyes that might even be panic. But there's more to it too. Fear. Raging lust, to the point where I almost blush. It occurs to me that all I'm wearing is a bikini. He's staring at me. Like, *all* of me. Everywhere. My face. My breasts, which are still wet from sitting in the hot tub. My legs. But then, there are the other layers to his emotion that kind of override all that. Sadness. Hopelessness. Regret.

I wish I could sit and talk with him for a while. To tell him that everything will be okay. That it might eventually be *more* than okay. Amazing, even.

But he turns and walks away, through the glass hallway that connects the pool area to the rest of the house, disappearing.

"Yikes," whispers Millie. "I think he might want to be alone. Maybe we should go."

"He probably needs some time to adjust to being back in his old life," I agree.

Millie messages Bo to tell him we're going back to our dorm, that Caleb is home and that she'll see him later.

As we're walking out to my car, I see movement in an upstairs window. Someone's standing there, watching me.

It's him.

He's taken off his shirt. *Jesus H. Christ.* He's *ludicrously* built. He stares at me for a few seconds like he's momentarily riveted. I wave and smile—as calmly and in as much of a non-OTT way as I'm capable of—but the curtains close.

We drive down the driveway and through the gates of the estate, out onto the tree-lined street. I turn the corner and stop at the stop sign.

Millie and I glance at each other but we don't say much. I think we're both remembering that look on his face. The darkness there and the obvious, heavy turmoil. "He didn't look injured," Millie comments.

"His outer injuries must be healing." But she's right. Caleb McCabe looked like a virile, pumped-up A-list specimen of prime and perfect masculinity. Only his eyes told a different story, hinting at a tip of some vast iceberg of emotion that draws me to Caleb McCabe even more than the beefcake drop-dead gorgeousness.

God.

I should forget about him. Distance myself. He'd clearly be a complicated and possibly terrible person to get involved with.

Involved with, Violet? Listen to yourself. He's a mess, and judging from his reaction to you, very much not interested. He obviously wants to be left alone.

But maybe I could … help him.

Like I couldn't help Joe.

Some guys pull up next to us in a pick-up truck and honk the horn. One of them lowers his window. "Hey, beautiful!" he yells, since my windows are up and staying that way. "Can I get your number?"

The light turns green so I peel out. They follow us for a while, but I take a short cut back to campus and we manage to lose them. You don't grow up with three (four) car-mad older brothers without learning how to drive like an Indy 500 champion.

Millie's clutching the side of the car but she doesn't tell me to slow down. "That was that guy from my American Literature class," she says. "He's actually nice."

"He is?" I look over at her. Is she suggesting what I think she's suggesting? "Then maybe you should date him."

We laugh.

Bo would go insane.

She doesn't say anything else and we let the topic slide. It's true I haven't been out on a date since I got to college. And I *do* want to start dating, of course I do. That's partly why I moved so far away from my brothers, so they wouldn't try to oversee my choices or threaten people they didn't think were good enough for me, which included everyone in my high school.

But I'm not interested in the guy from Millie's American Literature class. Suddenly, there's only one thing I'm interested in.

That thing happens to be a burly, beautiful, messed-up combat hero.

Caleb McCabe, I'll give you some time to adjust. But like it or not, you're my new mission. I lost someone I loved more than anything a long time ago, because I didn't know how to help him. But now, just maybe, I might be able to help you. I'm fun, I'm careful, and I'm going to coax you back into daylight.

If you'll let me.

4

CALEB

A HINT OF MOVEMENT. A shadow. A ghost.

I take aim. I'm ready to take my shot. Three of my men are advancing. It's up to me to take out any spooks that could get to them first.

Identify your target is Rule Number One, and even though my intuition is telling me to be aware, to watch that almost-undetectable flicker inside the small open window at the top left corner of the desecrated building, I can't see my target. It could be a child. Or the flutter of a torn, dirty curtain.

But then, the glint of sunlight on metal. The barrel of a rifle.

I fire and see the splatter of blood but it's too late. The bullets have already found their target.

Logan takes a direct hit and falls in that way that means he's dead before he even hits the ground.

No. Please no.

This is my fault, of course. I should have trusted my gut. I should have followed my instincts and done it anyway.

And now he's gone and his blood is all over my hands.

There's so fucking much *of it.*

This is a stain that won't ever come off. How could it? This will forever taint everything about me, all the way down to the depths of my wrecked and twisted soul.

It should have been me.

"Caleb? *Caleb.*"

I jerk awake.

Where the fuck am I? Where's my rifle?

"It's Bo," he says. "You're home. Everything's okay, man."

"What?" Oh. It's Bo.

"You were having another nightmare."

Fuck.

"Come on," Bo says. "I'm making dinner. You've been asleep for three days. Come downstairs and have some food."

"No." I turn over and pull the sheets over my head. I need darkness. I need sleep.

What I need is oblivion.

I SLEEP FOR A LONG TIME.

My dreams are pretty fucked up for the first few nights.

By the end of the week, they become less of the wake-up-screaming variety and more of the wake-up-sweating variety, which is at least an improvement, possibly. Then again, *improvement* is a relative term. Some parts of hell aren't really an *improvement* to other parts of hell. It's still hell.

My brother eventually insists that I come down and have a swim and eat some real food. He says he'll pick me up and carry me downstairs if I don't walk.

I'd like to see him try.

But I haven't eaten much at all for almost a week and I realize I'm starving.

When I look out the window, I'm glad to see it's raining.

I put on some old clothes. Everything is too tight at this point but I find a few things that barely fit. A t-shirt and a pair of board shorts.

I go downstairs and make my way outside, for the first time in a week.

Bo is cooking steaks on the barbecue, under the roof overhang of the outdoor kitchen. The steaks smell fucking good.

After living in the desert for the past year, the cool, light rain feels like it's watering my soul, cheesy as that may sound. "I'm going for a swim in the lake," I tell him.

He nods, like he thinks it's a good idea.

It's warm, despite the rain. It must be early or mid-September, I can't quite remember. I haven't looked at a phone or the news or anything since I got home.

I walk down the path to the lake, ditching my t-shirt. I

dive off the dock. The water is cold but it feels good. Like it's washing off a layer of the grit and grime of the desert that has coated me, burned my eyes, left a taste in my mouth and dirtied my psyche for the past year. It's a gritty, ever-present dust that gets into your lungs and under your skin until you wonder if you'll ever feel clean again.

I just float there for a while, looking up at the sky.

It's been a long time since I appreciated the beauty of … well, *anything*, so I just float here, watching the clouds and feeling, for the first time in a year *not* like I'm getting ready to kill or die at any minute. Like I can, finally … not be on guard.

The tiny drops of rain on my face are refreshing. I wouldn't go so far as to say I feel better, but I at least feel like I can handle having my eyes open.

Of course my thoughts drift … even though I try to stop them.

To *her*.

The vision of her is burned into my brain, as though the memory was seared with a red-hot branding iron.

The copper-and-golden-haired girl with the freckles, in that tiny goddamn white bikini that showed off the tan of pretty much *every* inch of her perfect skin. Her little cherry nipples, poking gently against that wet, flimsy layer.

Fucking hell.

I stop myself. If I continue down *that* particular road, I'll be reduced to a mess of lust and rage and regret.

I probably scared her away anyway by not talking to them earlier, or last week, or whenever that was.

My stomach growls.

So I swim back to shore and walk up the small sandy beach that was trucked in from Cape Cod years ago because my mother spent her childhood summers there. My father used to go to insane lengths to please her, in every way he could think of. At the time I thought he was out of his mind. But now, for the first time, I almost understand it. Why not go out of your way to make her happy? Any day your time could be up. Any second, it could all be over. Why not create happiness in every way you're capable of, every chance you get, while you can?

That word again.

Happiness.

She radiated happiness. Like a golden drug you could get addicted to if you stood too close to her.

I grab my t-shirt and start walking up to the house.

It feels good to be *cool* and wet and clean. The air feels soft. The sun is hanging lower in the sky now.

"Dinner's up," Bo says as I walk inside.

We sit at the bar. He's put on a feast for us. Steaks with mushrooms and potatoes. Beer, even, which I haven't had in a while. I don't drink on duty, even at the commissary. I could never drown my sorrows, like so many people do. I'd rather have a beer when life looks good. These days, that sentiment has been non-existent. But tonight, what the hell. I survived.

Even though they didn't.

"Cheers, brother," Bo says, clinking his glass against mine. "Good to have you home and in one piece."

"Good to be here and in one piece."

He doesn't ask about anything. I'm so grateful for that. He just talks about football and Coach Evans—who's still a prick that manages to somehow get the results he wants. He talks about the players. Tyler and Kowalski and a lot of guys I know from before. Scores. Odds. Plays. Their chances for the season and so on.

It's good to just listen to him talk about stuff that once meant something to me. There's still a thread of connection to all of it, and it makes me feel more grounded than I have in a while.

Three beers and two steaks later, with the sun hanging low over the lake and painting everything reddish-gold—the exact same color as Violet's hair—I'm grasping at straws of actual normality. I'm not even close, but it's a start.

"So, tell me about Millie." I say. I really don't talk much these days. But with Bo, it's okay.

My younger brother, I notice now, has beefed up a lot over the past year. Damn, he looks a lot like my father. More now than he ever did. "She's the one," he says.

I knew about his "promise," of course. Those things he said to my mother as she was dying. About saving himself for the real thing. At first I thought it was a stunt to get even more girls to chase after him. Bo has never had trouble in that department and neither have I. But it turns out he meant every word of it.

"I first saw her on the big screen. There she was, this angel, just sort of *glowing*. She was like nothing I'd ever seen. I literally couldn't take my eyes off her. And now, when I'm not with her, I think I'm going to lose my fucking mind." He laughs a little and runs his hand through his hair. "Crazy, right?"

I think about what he just said. *She was like nothing I'd ever seen.* I'm trying *not* to think about the dreams I started having, after the nightmares started to rove into different territory. They still pummel me every night, but after almost four or five solid days of sleeping, I started having other dreams too … *of her* … in that fucking little white bikini. In my dreams, I don't walk away. I reach out and *take off* her bikini, as she smiles at me with those pink lips and those playful, flashing green eyes.

In fact, by about the sixth night, she'd started *taking over* my dreams, pushing my nightmares aside and changing their direction. Mostly, those dreams were sweet. The ones where she's willing.

But there were others too. When I'm not so gentle. *When the lust becomes dark-edged … when I'll do absolutely anything to have her.*

With effort, I stay focused. "Where is she tonight?"

"She has a late class. Are you up for a few people coming around tomorrow? A few of the guys want to see you."

People? Here?

Of course I wonder if *she'll* be coming.

I want to see her again. Just to watch her, to see if she's as beautiful as I remember her. I can't guarantee I'll speak to her. I don't even know if I *want* to speak to her. Speaking to her would be dangerous. I'd be too tempted to sling her over my shoulder and carry her away to some secluded place ...

I don't trust myself to be anywhere near that girl. I don't feel stable enough to have a conversation with her, let alone anything else.

"I ... yeah," I bluff. "No problem. It's fine."

Anyway, she probably wouldn't be interested. After our last meeting, she probably thinks I'm a socially stunted freak or a psycho. Which wouldn't be wrong.

I feel more rested now. I've eaten a good meal. I've had a beer and a swim. Like this, it'll be fine. I can sit in some peripheral chair and disappear if I need to.

"I'm going to move into the lake house tomorrow." I tip back the last of my drink.

"I thought you might," Bo says. "It's quieter. But it might be good to catch up with a few people first, right? Start socializing a little and reacclimatizing?"

I can tell he's worried about how disengaged I am. I've changed, that's obvious. "Sure."

I'll be fine. I'll start to reconcile the fact that loud voices and sharp noises don't mean someone's shooting at us.

I'll make a point of remembering that the neighbors

aren't highly trained snipers with assault rifles pointing directly at my head.

I'll appreciate the peaceful night and not get paranoid or weird or hostile to the point of hurting someone or freaking the fuck out or acting like a card-carrying lunatic.

Sure I can.

I can handle it.

5

Violet

IT'S BEEN about a week since I ran into Caleb McCabe. I'm slightly annoyed by how insistently he's taken up residence in my thoughts. I can't *stop* thinking about him. His *face*, like a rugged movie star who'd just stepped off set. His hair, dark and all glamorously mussed-up. *His body*, holy hell, don't even get me started.

I wish I could forget about him, and get on with my carefree, low-drama, non-obsessed-with-a-rude-and-reclusive-stranger life. I've asked a few casual questions, and Millie told me he's basically been holed up at his house sleeping since he got home.

Which is good. Sleep can cure a lot of problems.

But not all problems.

I'm just getting out of my Personality class when my phone rings. *Millie* lights up the screen.

"Hey, Millz."

"Bo's having some people over tonight. Mostly football players. Come with me."

I try to be subtle about it but subtlety isn't exactly my strong point. "Have you, um, seen Caleb since that first time?" I try to contain … I don't know. Excitement? Fear? Lust? *Definitely lust.* Even now, just thinking about that charged, brief encounter, I feel a flush rise to my skin, like even from all the way over there, he's capable of touching me with his crazy magnetism. I decide it's not fear. I'm not scared of Caleb McCabe. The only thing I'm scared of is the possibility that I might not be able to help him, if he even needs help. Then again, I'll never know unless I try.

"No," says Millie. "Bo said he's moving into the lake house."

"Oh." Is that a good idea? For him to be living alone?

I've been reading a lot about PTSD, partly because it's my homework, but mostly … because of a certain ultra-sexy soldier I met the other day who wouldn't even speak to me.

There are four main behaviors associated with post-traumatic stress disorder: avoidance (like avoiding situations that remind you of the event and also, possibly … not talking to people even when they say hi to you), intrusive memories (like re-living the event day to day or having nightmares), negative changes in mood (like basically being rude to people you just met because you're so wrapped up in your memories), and changes in physical and emotional reactions (like being irritable or always on guard … or being a total jerk to someone because you sort of can't help it).

Not that I'm trying to be his savior or anything, but I've been thinking about things I might be able do for Caleb that might be the tiniest bit helpful. I've started writing a list:

- 1) ask him if he's in therapy; if not, encourage him (gently!! he might get pissed off because we already know he's very irritable!!!) to start going
- 2) help him think positive thoughts about himself and the world in general (yay, my specialty!!!)
- 3) talk to him (carefully!!) about self-care, getting enough rest, eating healthy food, exercising, doing things he used to enjoy doing, doing things that make him feel good etc. (yay again!: talking through all this stuff is also something I'm fabulous at, just sayin'!!)

So, if Caleb *is* at the party tonight, at least I have a plan in place for things to talk about—I mean, if we get a quiet place to talk one on one. That is, *if* he'll even talk to me at all. Which is, of course, a big if.

"I have to go see one of my professors about an assignment," Millie tells me. "I'll meet you back at the room in an hour."

"Okay, see you then."

"Hey, Violet," someone says to me just as I'm ending the call. It's a guy in my class.

I look up at him as I slide my phone into my back pocket. "Oh. Hey." I can't remember his name.

"Josh," he smiles. He's an inch or two taller than me and has sandy brown hair. His slim, friendly boyishness clashes with my omnipresent memories of Caleb McCabe's stormy, beefed-up masculinity. "Did you finish the assignment due tomorrow?"

"Oh. Yeah." I don't mention I finished it the night after our professor assigned it. As I mentioned, I have a problem.

"I haven't even started it yet," he says. "Do you want to get together tonight and go through what you've written?"

"Um, I can't. Sorry, I've got plans."

"How about tomorrow night, then? It's not due until Monday."

I can picture what a nice, easy relationship with someone like Josh would be like. He's a freshman, like me. He's young and open and seems well-adjusted. We could do our assignments together. He'd be kind and accommodating and we'd take things slow. He wouldn't rush me or upset me or push me too hard.

Which, in this moment, feels about as appealing as an ice cold shower.

I hate to admit that Caleb McCabe has lit some warm, glowing ember in me that I can't seem to shake or avoid or dim down. Every recall of his wild eyes and his crazy appeal only stokes it.

I need to get a grip.

I've never had anything like this happen before and it's

unnerving. Like a piece of him has lodged itself inside me and won't leave. I know for a fact that if I do see Caleb again—and I feverishly *want* to with a vehemence that alarms me a little—it'll be rough seas, layered glares, clashes of wills and the kind of heat I could never have with someone like Josh.

I'm not going to say I've *fallen* for Caleb during that brief, silent, one-minute encounter, not at all. I mean, that would be ridiculous. I don't know how to define what I'm feeling. All I know is that I want to do it again. But, this time, maybe with words. Or a smile, even.

I wonder what Caleb McCabe looks like when he smiles. I bet he's even more heartbreakingly beautiful than the sullen glare. I wonder what his laughter sounds like. I wonder how strong his grip is.

Jesus. I'm totally losing it.

"Maybe another time, Josh," I say, even though I know it won't happen. "I've … my schedule is really busy at the moment."

"Sure." His disappointment is calm and forgiving. "Can I get your number? Maybe we could get together next week."

"Oh. I'll just … I'll see you in class on Monday. We can talk then." We can have bland, gentle conversations that lead nowhere and leave me feeling annoyed and dissatisfied.

Hell, Violet. Maybe you could give the guy a chance before dismissing him because he's nice.

But I can't.

Because I've tasted *passion*, I think, when I was least

expecting it. Is *that* what that was? One minute—or less—was all it took to make me understand that I want something more than safety and easy nothingness. *How is that even possible?*

I don't know. All I do know is that I want another minute. And then one more.

I want to feel that wild vibe he gave off again.

I want to *feel.* Anything at all.

I want to feel what he *has to give me.*

It doesn't make any sense but I'm walking away from Josh, giving him a little wave as I make my escape, already thinking about tonight, and what might, maybe—or maybe not—happen.

"THAT OUTFIT IS SO CUTE." Millie has white jeans on and a cute pink top that makes her look like even more gorgeous than usual. With her long, pink-blond hair, she basically looks like a goddess that just flew in from Mount Olympus.

"So's yours," she says. I'm wearing a white cotton sundress with long sleeves that I bought just the other day. We both have our bikinis on underneath, since we'll probably end up spending some time in the hot tub.

We drive over to Bo's house and Millie lets us in with the app Bo installed on her phone. There are already around ten cars parked out front. Bo opens the door, and as soon as he sees Millie, he scoops her into his arms and starts kissing her like he forgot they're in public. She squirms and scolds him for getting carried away, which he always does when it comes to Millie. When he finally puts her down, she's blushing. "I missed you," Bo gushes, then, noticing me, "Hey, Violet." He grins at me.

"Hey, Bo." He gently fist-pumps me, which has become this thing we do.

Bo introduces us to some of the people. Football players, mostly. Plus a few other friends. Luckily, since I grew up in the constant company of people exactly like them, it's easy to talk to them and I end up meeting a few new people. I've met some of them before, like Tyler, a linebacker, and Hayes, a wide receiver, who has blond hair and, despite the fact that no less than three girls are literally hanging off him, winks at me.

Caleb is nowhere to be seen.

A sane person would chase after one of these happy-go-lucky football players and be done with it.

But I know better than most that sanity is a loose term. Everyone's got issues. Everyone's got areas where they're walking a thin line.

I talk to Hayes and his groupies for a while, then I walk out onto the back patio where a lot more people are hanging out. The sliding doors into the pool area have been opened. It's a warm night. A few people are already sitting in the hot tub. Music is playing and a few guys are cooking at the barbecue. There are platters on the tables, full of food.

I see Caleb laying on one of the loungers at the far end of the patio. He's wearing sunglasses, a black t-shirt and a pair of jeans. He's barefoot. He's alone and seems to like it that way. He might even be asleep.

I decide not to go over and launch into my I'm-going-to-save-you-and-solve-all-your-problems conversation (yet). Bo has invited us to stay the night so we can have a drink or two, so when someone hands me a glass of champagne, I take it.

Millie and I talk for a while to a girl named Jess who's in two of my psych classes. I watch as a couple of the football groupies walk over to where Caleb is sitting. They're dressed in skimpy dresses that are skin-tight and low cut. They sit down on the loungers next to his.

They're trying to talk to him. They're flipping their hair and giggling, but he doesn't even seem to acknowledge them. His sunglasses are dark and his burly arms are folded across his chest.

Is he okay? Is he feeling anxious? Overwhelmed? Panicked? Depressed?

I have the urge to protect him from their banal small talk.

Before I can, the two girls stand up. They're offended by something he's said to them. They walk away in a huff and give him dirty looks before going back inside the house.

I guess that settles it.

Caleb wants to be left alone.

Changes in physical and emotional reactions: check. *Irritability and aggressive, sometimes-irrational behavior:* check.

If I go over there, he'll probably shut me down like he did to those other girls.

Or not. Something about the way he looked at me, when we first met and also from the bedroom window … it makes me think that maybe he would talk to me. Like maybe *I* could be the one to get through to him …

Get over yourself, Violet. You're not a miracle worker or even a qualified shrink yet. He doesn't want to talk, to you or anyone else, that's obvious.

I'm almost glad when Millie interrupts my thoughts and asks me to sit it the hot tub with her, so we go into the pool area and strip down to our bikinis. Hayes joins us and we talk and laugh for a while. Hayes casually rests his burly arm behind my shoulders along the rim of the hot tub. His blond hair brushes against my cheek as he leans closer.

"What are you studying, Violet?" His solid, hairy thigh grazes mine. He's grinning at me sort of cockily, like football players tend to do.

"Psychology." I ease my leg away from his. "Nice touchdown catch in the last three seconds of the game last weekend, by the way."

"Thanks." I know all about Hayes's plays, stats and tendencies on the field. It's a hangover from all those years of watching my brothers. I can't help myself, I just sort of drink in the details. I know Hayes is just a little too slow to be a hot pick for the NFL, that his catch last weekend was a lucky score and had more to do with a missed offensive tackle and a textbook-perfect pass from Bo than Hayes's skills on the field, but I don't say it.

Hayes is a nice enough guy, but he's not really my type. Not that I know what my type actually *is*, to be honest. Having three (four) older brothers who were gigantic, muscular superstars throughout my teenage years tended to mean the high school dating scene was less than stellar. My brother Henry actually admitted to me once that all three of them threatened to beat to a pulp any guy who touched me. I was furious when I found out about that, but it didn't change anything. Which means I've had a lot of friends who are boys, but not a single boyfriend.

Even though I love them to pieces, when the time came to apply for colleges, I decided to put at least several states between me and my brothers in the interest of having an actual love life one of these days. So I applied to several schools further afar, got early acceptance to my first choice and that was that.

The two girls who tried to talk to Caleb earlier slide into the hot tub. They start talking to Hayes and I take that as my cue. I climb out and wrap a towel around my waist.

I notice then that Caleb is gone. I catch a glimpse of him walking down to the dock house. Next to it, there's a very large boat lift but the boat has been lowered and is tied up next to the dock. Caleb disappears.

I panic a little. Is he having some of those negative

thoughts I was reading about? Some people suffering from PTSD have recurring self-destructive thoughts.

God, I hope he's not ... I'm sure he wouldn't ... *would he?*

(No one ever expected Joe to do that either.)

I decide to follow him. I want to make sure he's okay. I grab my dress and slip it over my head, but my bikini is still wet so it clings to me.

The sun is low now, touching the horizon, painting the water a brilliant shade of orange.

As I get closer, I can see Caleb sitting in one of the chairs at the end of the covered area of the dock. I'm barefoot, but I make sure my footsteps aren't too soft, so he can hear me coming. I don't want to startle him.

For a second I feel the tiniest flicker of fear. Will he be mad?

I can take rudeness, but ... is it possible that he'll be angry? *Or aggressive?* For a second I wonder if this was a good idea.

We're alone out here. Once I retreat inside the covered dock, no one will be able to see us.

I almost turn back.

But I don't.

Because of my *own* damages. Caleb McCabe, whether I like it or not, is like a magnet to me. His vulnerabilities. Those shadows behind his eyes.

I've seen those shadows before. In the eyes of my beautiful brother.

For better or worse, I happen to be a person who, once I

set my mind to something, I'm basically unswayable, second thoughts or no second thoughts.

We'll be completely alone.

The music coming from the house is louder now.

No one will be able to hear you.

I do it anyway.

I step into the dock house.

You have no idea how he'll react to you.

I guess I'm about to find out.

6

CALEB

I CAN BARELY TOLERATE BEING around these people. Their casual loudness and their idiotic banter. Their mindless fun. It's an outlook I can't relate to anymore. I do my best to tune out.

Logan was always the life of the party. If I'd fired that shot one fucking second earlier, he'd be here now, cracking jokes. I wonder if they scooped up his brains and shipped them home along with the rest of him. Why him and not me? Why Connor? Or Quinn, who cried for his mother as he lay dying? Why do I get to live and they don't? It doesn't make sense. They were better people than I am or ever will be.

I try to shut down those particular trains of thought. They only take me on a one-way trip to hell station, a place I'd prefer to avoid, at least for the next five minutes.

I'm only here because *she* might be coming. I want to

look at her one more time before I retreat to the quiet darkness. Maybe I was wrong. Maybe the sight of her won't hit me like a ton of bricks this time. Maybe then I can move on and forget about her.

It would be nice not to have my dreams haunted, or, more accurately, charmed and fucking *enchanted*, by her ... until my dream-self destroys her. But then again, she's basically given me something to live for, as pathetic as that might sound.

She steps out onto the patio area and my annihilation is complete. I'm a goner.

She's wearing a white dress that's not tight-fitting but still hints at the lines of her insanely luscious body, slim but curvy in all the right places. Her long legs are bare and tanned and she's wearing high heeled sandals. Her hair hangs loose around her shoulders and down her back like a fine-spun spilling halo of bright reds and golds. She's wearing pink lip gloss, a detail I wouldn't usually notice, but her lips are so insanely tantalizing, she's making my mouth water.

Fucking hell.

Her gaze finds me right away and I'm glad I'm wearing dark glasses. I don't want her to feel my hot stare, but maybe she does anyway because, for a second, she holds it. But then it drifts like she's not sure if I'm awake or asleep.

I'm a million miles from sleep.

They're all watching her, of course. She's lighting up the

entire party. She's by far the most beautiful girl I've ever seen, by a country mile.

A couple of chicks come over cautiously. They sit next to me and it pisses me off that they would intrude on my concentration of her. I have to stop myself from telling them to fuck off. They're not ugly. They're just not *her*. And I'm barely me.

"You must be Bo's brother," one of them says.

"We heard you just got back from a war," the other one says. "That must have been *so* scary!"

"Did you ever, like, *kill* anyone?" says the other one, and I can't handle this.

"Please," I tell them, using every ounce of self-control I have. "Leave me alone. Go away. Now. Or there's no telling what I might do."

They both stare at me, hurt. And maybe even scared.

Good. They should be scared. I feel mean. And dangerous. I shouldn't be here, hanging out around normal people having a good time.

They stand up—and this relieves me outrageously. Then they skulk away like I'm a total asshole, and maybe I am, but I can't quite bring myself to care about that. As soon as they're back in the crowd, my heartbeat begins to almost normalize. But not quite.

Violet is talking to a few people. She's friendly. Cute as fuck. Completely un-self-conscious. Aware, maybe, of that inner beauty she radiates.

As for her *outer* beauty, it's off the fucking charts. It's blowing my goddamn head off.

She goes into the pool area and takes off her dress and I think I might lose my mind. Today, her bikini is pink and might even be skimpier than the last one. Her hair is shiny and bouncy like a shampoo commercial. There's a sprinkling of golden freckles across her shoulders. She's so fucking gorgeous it hurts.

Of course they're staring. Hayes, that overrated tryhard. His eyes are practically popping out of his head. He climbs into the hot tub next to her, attempting to put his arm around her.

I'll fucking kill him.

No. You won't. You'll let her choose one of them. Someone safe and stable and sane. Someone who won't totally fuck up her life.

If I have to watch one more second of this, I'm going to do something I'll probably regret. Am I capable of self-control? Maybe. Is it more likely that I'll storm over there and punch him in the face if I have to watch even one more milli-second of him drooling all over the most perfect girl in the goddamn world?

Yes.

Would *I* be in that hot tub asking her to choose *me* instead if I thought there was even the remotest chance I wouldn't break her heart and destroy her life?

Yes.

There's no way I'm going to dirty her life with my damages.

I need to get the fuck away from here.

Someone has turned the music up. The vibrations of the bass remind me of bomb detonations and shrapnel wounds. Blood. Mutilated bodies.

It's painful. The overcast late afternoon has become desolate and shadowed around me. Is there any point in even being a part of this life anymore? Everything about this re-entry into the civilian world feels too heavy. I'm really not sure I can bear it.

The thought of pushing my way through the crowded patio makes me feel like I'm going to be sick. So I walk out the other way, through the archway and down the steps to the dock, which is—thank fuck—clear. It'll be quiet down there. I'll be all alone, which is exactly what I need. I'll watch the sunset. If I see someone coming, I'll jump on the boat. Anchor it out somewhere in the middle of the lake and just lay there for the rest of the week.

Suck it up, soldier. You're alive and they're dead. Honor their memory by making the most of the life you got to keep.

Sure.

I know. I'm trying. Or, more accurately, I will try. One day. If I can get through the fog and the darkness.

I'm sweating and my skin feels clammy so I take off my shirt. I sit in one of the cushiony, reclining loungers and look out at the view. The lake. The rolling hills. The scattered clouds and the colors of the sunset.

This is better. The laughter is far away now, the music less intense.

Is she talking to him? Is he touching her hair?

I don't know if I can do it. I don't know if I can leave her alone. It would be so easy to storm back up there and beat Hayes to a bloody pulp. He'd never even see it coming.

I force myself to stay in my chair. I take a deep breath. *Calm down, man. Don't overreact.*

Just as I'm starting to feel less like I'm about to kill or strangle the next person who talks to me, I hear footsteps.

I turn, ready to … then I see who it is.

Holy fuck, it's her.

Just her.

She's in her white dress, which is clinging to her wet body and her pink bikini underneath. *Jesus.* Her vibrant hair seems to catch all the light of the sunset. I stand up, and again I notice how small she is, how outrageously … *feminine*, with those lush curves and all that ludicrous softness.

"Caleb?" she says cautiously. "I'm sorry to bother you. I saw you leave and I just … wanted to make sure you were okay." Her accent has a Southern twang to it that makes my cock go instantly fucking rock-hard.

Fuck.

I'll do better this time. I won't freak out like a fucking lunatic, even though I'm sure I qualify. So I start with, "It's fine."

"I can leave if you don't want company. I just thought … I wanted to make sure you were okay," she says again.

"It's no problem." Not exactly profound, but at least I'm able to speak this time. If it was anyone else, it's hard to say whether my fight or flight reflex would win. With her, I feel neither of these urges. I *want* her here. Her presence feels like a cool balm against the raging heat of my torment. "Do you … want to sit?"

She tentatively sits. I sit next to her. Her dress is clinging wetly to her body as she sits back on the lounger. Her breasts are full and her nipples are poking against the thin, damp fabric. The hem of her dress lays high on her thighs and flush against her body. As her legs part, I can almost see the soft, swelled outline of her pussy.

Holy fuck. I can't take this. She's so fucking beautiful.

My cock starts to throb. Even worse, my body starts to feel alive in a way it hasn't in a very long time.

"Are you … okay?" she asks.

With her sitting here with me, I almost feel like I am. Her presence buffers away degrees of the pain. For a few blissful seconds, her sweet, wet beauty is the only thing I'm aware of. All the memories fade back, overpowered by Violet's damp skin, her pink, parted lips, the shape of her nipples and the way her dress is clinging to the round, taut little peaks. It's impossible: I'll never be able to resist her. I'll never be able to walk away.

"How's the party going?" I manage.

"It's fine. But this is better."

I have no idea how it could be. "I saw you talking to Hayes up there." *Why would you bring that up, you fucking idiot?* To find out. Maybe she's dating him or something. I need to know. *So I can smash his face in.*

"Hayes? Oh. Yeah. He's nice, but I think he flirts with every single girl he meets. I could never be interested in someone like Hayes."

"Oh yeah? Why not?" I might actually be having a conversation here. It's the first one I've had in a while with someone other than Bo and it's … nice. I don't just want to *handle* it, I want to make it last.

"He's not my type." She points out to the horizon. "Look. There goes the last of the sun. Make a wish."

A wish.

For her, I do make a wish. *Please let me be strong enough to handle getting close to this girl.*

I can't help myself. I make another wish. *Please let me taste every inch of that sweet, wet body until she's begging me for more.*

And I can't stop myself from asking her, "What's your type, then?"

"I have no idea," she says, then she laughs. I can honestly say her laughter is the most beguiling sound I've ever heard in my life. I could even say it gives me hope. Because I want to hear it again. And again.

My cock is agonizingly hard, which is probably totally obvious. Ten inches isn't really something you can hide, even in the fading daylight. But, hell, if she's going to come all the way down here and sit next to me with that thin wet dress clinging to her spectacular body, that's a risk she's going to take.

Fuck, I haven't had a hard-on like *this* for a while. And I can't tell if she's aware yet of the effect she's having on me, or of how engorged and thick I've become, or how the tip of my cock is practically on the verge of sticking out of my jeans and is well on its way to spilling a torrential flood of hot cum. *All over her.*

Calm the fuck down, boy.

"I hope you've caught up on your rest and relaxation a little," she says, staring out at the dazzling final moments of the sunset.

"That's all I've done. I slept for six solid days."

"Wow, you must have been pretty tired." She glances over at me. She's so gorgeous, all I really want to do is kiss her, to suck on her, to feed on all that beauty. I feel fucking *voracious* with hot, hungry lust. She smiles gently. "I always think everything feels better and brighter and more optimistic when I get a good night's sleep."

I catch her gaze and a warmth passes between us that almost calms me. *Fuck.* She's like some kind of tonic. Her nearness is revving me up and at the same time soothing me in a way that's new and more than a little addictive. "It sure does today," I tell her, and it's true, not because I've caught up on sleep, but because Violet is sitting here with me, with her hair spilling over her shoulders, laying silkily against her arms, framing those full breasts with their teasing little nipples poking out at me, like they're asking for it. It would be so easy to reach over and ease her dress lower—

"I'm sure you have a lot of friends," she says, "but I just want to say that if you ever want to talk or just spend time with someone, you could … you know, call me. If you wanted to. Anytime."

"Thanks." It's a nice offer. I can see what she's doing, prodding at my issues, and that's cool. With her, it feels okay. So I say the most honest thing I can think of. "You're the first person I've wanted to spend time with. In fact, you're the *only* person I want to spend time with."

Her eyes are bright in the fading light. The night is warm and humid. She smiles again. "I want to spend time with you too, Caleb. I've been thinking about you all week."

"I'm sorry about that first time. I wasn't myself."

"You don't have to explain anything. It's okay."

What I should do right now is to politely tell her I have somewhere I need to be, and walk away. If I can only cope with reality by sleeping for a week and distancing myself from everyone, there's no way in hell I can handle a relationship. Especially with someone like *this* … this vibrant, stunning girl.

She's *too* beautiful … and too *luscious*, her lips like a ripe fruit. The *shape* of her outrageous body is hypnotizing me. I want to kiss her. I want to lick that sweet mouth. I want to ease her back on that reclining lounger, take off her dress and rip that little bikini off with my teeth.

Walk away, Caleb. You're not ready for this. All you'll do is drag her down into the twisted quagmire of your jaded mess of a soul. You'll hurt her. You'll do things to her that will be dark and extreme. Get away from her. You're too fucked up for someone so undamaged and pure.

I almost do it. I almost stand up. I almost save her from myself.

But then I hear voices.

Fucking hell. Some people are on the track, coming down here. Getting closer.

A bloom of rage kickstarts my heart. I do *not* want to be around people—people that aren't Violet—at all. If I have to make small talk about war or what caliber rifles we used or what my strike rate is or where did the shrapnel tear my flesh and did it hurt or any of those other inane questions people ask, I'll lose my fucking mind.

The boat.

"Listen," I say, "I'm going to take the boat out for a spin, get some fresh air." I sound strange. I feel strange. I glance back up the hill and I can see two girls making their way down the path. Those same fucking ones.

Did you ever, like, kill anyone?

Yes, honey. My tally stands at sixty-nine confirmed kills. What a statistic to be proud of, don't you think? I cried real tears after the first four. It's true. Because can you imagine how it feels to do that? To take another person's life like that? It's a brutal thing to live with. You can't help thinking about their families and their mothers and their fatherless children. But after the first few, something in me turned. To grit. Because it was a part of my job description and it was them or it was us. Even so, every now and then, I hesitated. Like one day, not too long ago, when I should have trusted my instincts and taken the shot. And you know what? It cost my best friend his life. One bullet hit him right between the eyes and—well,

I'll spare you the most gruesome details because it hurts to think about it, let alone describe it. But I can tell you he was the best person I knew. What do you think about that, honey? Have I ruined your party mood yet?

Fucking Hayes is with the girls, I notice.

I step onto the boat and I feel a light touch on my arm. I almost flinch, but she's so small compared to me, so pink and soft with that dazzling hair and that cute-as-fuck face. She's staring up at me, concerned. "Caleb, are you okay?"

"Fine." *Don't ask. Don't ask.* But before I can stop myself, I hear myself say it anyway: "Want to come?" As if I'm going to leave her here with Hayes.

She hesitates for a second, and I'm almost glad for that. *Walk away, Violet. Run. Keep your distance or I'll drag you down here into the fires of hell right alongside me.*

Because I know for a fact that if she comes with me I won't be able to resist her. If I'm stuck out on the boat with her with its wide couches on deck and its berth down below, cool and comfortable and hidden away from the world, I know I won't be able to control the building, violent hunger that's like nothing I've ever experienced.

Another gift from my father to my mother. *Sweet Caroline.* Her name. A twenty-foot yacht, for our lake, with a romantic little seating area on deck and a plush bedroom down below so he could take her sailing whenever he wanted. So they had an escape from the rest of the world whenever they needed it, they could anchor themselves out here and no one could reach them.

Dad, strangely, I understand you better right now than I ever did when you were alive.

I never understood his obsession or his devotion.

Suddenly, I do.

And if she steps on board with me, I know I won't be able to stop until I've tasted every inch of this golden girl and made her come and come and marked every piece of her with my dark lust and my voracious, primal need.

"Okay," she says lightly.

7

I ALMOST SAY NO.

Is it safe to be alone with him?

But I don't say no. Of course I don't. First, I don't want him to be alone, either. He shouldn't be alone. He's suffering from his symptoms, I can see that. And at least he's talking to me now, which might be a step in the right direction. Talking is good. Talking helps. As for the other reason, *sweet Jesus, he's hot. And hard. And huge.* Of course *I noticed it!* It was impossible not to.

Which freaks me out. But I don't feel scared of him, even if I should. I feel like being careful with him. I want to make sure he's okay and not on the brink of doing something reckless.

So I climb onto the small yacht—which is incredibly

cute and amazing—even though I'm a little nervous about this.

We pull away from the dock and Hayes hollers something from land, which I can't hear.

It'll be fine. We'll cruise around the lake for a while, we'll talk a little more and I'll remind Caleb about some positives so he can look on the bright side for an hour or two, then we'll get back to the house and the party will be winding down and we'll hang out with Bo and Millie before bed. We'll have a nice time together, I'll make sure of it. I'll distract him from his worries.

We get further from shore. This lake is actually a lot bigger than it looked from the house. We sail for a while and Caleb steers us around a bend that takes us into a secluded cove that's surrounded by trees. I'm sitting on one of the cushioned seats under a jutting roof at the bow. It's a beautiful evening. Daylight has faded to violet, with only the waning golden glow at the base of the horizon. The moon is already out and its reflection shimmers in the silver mirror of the water. The air is unseasonably warm for the end of September.

We slow to a stop and Caleb anchors the yacht.

He adjusts some ropes and gauges. He glances over at me. "You all right?"

His eyes are dark. All he's wearing is a low-slung pair of worn jeans. His muscles ripple and bulge as he moves. He has a tattoo of a pair of wings across his back. I can vaguely see the pink and silver marks of his scars on his stomach and chest. There are a lot of them. *Shrapnel,* I remember Millie saying something about. He's still healing from his injuries.

"Yeah," I say. "Are you?"

"Better now." It's good that he can be honest like that.

I decide to try to gently keep him talking. "Caleb, you know things will keep getting better, right? Like now. It's so beautiful out here, don't you think? Look, the stars are starting to come out." A little trite, maybe, but my goal is to point out things that might make him feel hopeful and positive and good about himself and the world in general. "This view is amazing. And *you* … are so … amazingly … fit." Oops. Where was I going with this?

He looks over at me and if I didn't know better, I'd almost say he almost seems like he's … not quite smiling, but is at least capable of it. "Thanks."

"I bet you work out a lot." *Jesus, Violet. Is that the best you can do here?*

He exhales—and, *yes!* It's almost a laugh. But not quite. "As a matter of fact, I do. It helps keep me sane, or close enough."

"Well, it's really paying off." *Holy shit.* My brain has turned to mush. It's just that it's sort of hard to think about how to best counsel a person who's so … *freaking … hot.*

He comes over and sits down next to me. His eyes are the darkest shade of blue. The muscles of his neck are corded and tan. His shoulders are impossibly wide and strong-looking. We sit there like that for a while and it's nice. The silence doesn't feel awkward or tense so I let him acclimatize to the calmness and drink it in. I bet he hasn't seen a lot of calmness in the last year. He seems like he needs it.

"So, you grew up here?" I finally ask.

"Yeah," he says, looking over at me. "My parents were both from Chicago. I was born there but we moved here when I was around four. They bought this property and built everything that's here. What about you?"

"North Carolina. Wilmington. It's where I've lived my whole life. In the same house."

"I spent some time at Camp Lejeune during my training, the summer before my senior year."

"Really? That's so close to where I live. It's only around ten minutes away from my house."

After a while he says, "To think that we were so close to each other." His voice is low and has that husky edge to it that's basically the most alluring sound I've ever heard in my life. It's that detail, along with the violet eyes and the hard muscles and the deep, dark vulnerabilities buried under all the sexy, tough-guy exterior ... well, the entire cocktail is making me fall just a little bit in love with Caleb McCabe.

Which is outrageous.

I've never been in love. I've never even been in *like*. My brothers wouldn't allow me to get that far. All the boys in my high school were scared to come near me. Which is probably why I'm having this overblown reaction to the first hot guy I've basically ever been alone with.

Caleb might be traumatized by violence beyond the scope of anything I can even imagine. But one thing he doesn't seem scared of is being close to me. His warm, incredibly hard, jean-clad thigh is resting next to my bare one.

I try to tone down my fascination, but it's no use. He's stunningly masculine and just … overwhelmingly beautiful. I can't seem to stop staring at him. "Maybe we ran into each other somewhere."

"No way," he says. "I would have remembered that."

I laugh lightly. "Not necessarily."

"Trust me, I would have."

"When did you spend time in North Carolina?"

"Around two and a half years ago. Almost three years now. I trained while I studied. I graduated as a Lance Corporal in the Marines and went to Quantico the following summer, before I was deployed."

So he must be twenty-three or twenty-four. "What do you do in the Marines?"

"I'm a Scout Sniper."

"A sniper? Is that when … ?" Of course it is.

"Yes. I'm a very good shot."

Wow. He shoots for a living. Or at least he used to. I don't want to dredge up the recent pain of his injuries and the difficulties of his time away so I try to steer him away from the topic. "What about before that? Before you joined the Marines? Bo mentioned that both his brothers went to the same university and played football. What did you study?"

"Economics. And finance."

I wonder if the magnitude of Caleb's gorgeousness will ever start to wear off, or to feel *less* mesmerizing. "Really?" I wouldn't have picked that. "Why finance?"

"I started investing in the stock market when I was, I don't know, maybe eight or nine years old. Our father taught us. He was a good teacher. He made it into a game and since all three of us are competitive as hell, we learned fast. By the time I was eighteen I was financially independent. But he said you could never know too much. So I got a degree in it."

"*Eighteen?* Then why did you join the Marines if you didn't need to?"

He sits back, contemplating the reflection of the moon on the water. "It was about finding a purpose, I guess. My parents had both just died, in ways that were terrible and tragic and life-changing for all three of us. I needed something else to think about."

He's talking to me. About things that matter. "And you used to play football?"

"Yeah. I was a quarterback."

"Like Bo."

"Like Bo. And Gage."

What do you know. A whole family of quarterbacks.

"What about you?" he says. "Are you a freshman?"

"Yes. I'm majoring in psychology."

There's a hint of humor to the glint in his eyes. "No kidding."

We're getting to know each other. Little by little, I'm

bringing Caleb McCabe out of his shell. *It's working.* He seems a degree less angst-ridden than he did earlier. Maybe I actually *can* help him, even if it's in small ways. Maybe it'll be enough to keep him off the metaphorical (or not so metaphorical) ledge. *Like I failed to do once before.*

"What's your last name?" he asks me.

"Jameson. Violet Aurora Jameson. I have three older brothers. And a dog named Earl."

He blinks thick lashes. "Earl?"

"Yes," I say defensively. "He's a bulldog."

"Who named Earl?"

"Me."

This time he actually does smile, and—*wow*—it feels like some kind of triumph. "Don't mock Earl," I say, but I can't help smiling back at him. His grin is roguish. His eyes are entrancing me.

And that's when two of his fingers swirl an end strand of my hair, ensnaring it in a light hold. "I would never do that to Earl," he murmurs.

It's the first time he's touched me.

"Your hair is so … colorful," he says. "And so are your eyes."

If my brain was already mush, this lightest touch and all the caged energy behind it has a very strange effect on me. My body feels warm. My heart is beating fast, and I can feel my pulse like a craving. "So are yours," is the only thing I can think of to say. It's true. This close, the blue of his eyes has inflections, not just of different, darker blues but of memories and feelings and ideas. It's riveting, how much depth his eyes have.

"I have this urge not to waste time," he says quietly.

"I can understand why you would."

"So I'm going to tell you what I'm thinking. I hope you don't mind."

"I don't mind. It's good to talk, Caleb. You can talk to me," I say, and I mean it, but I'm beginning to sense that there's a lot going on here, and I wonder if I can handle the *extent* of it.

"You fucking blew my mind that first time I saw you," he says, his voice low. "And every moment since. I have never seen anyone so beautiful."

Somewhere it occurs to me that this is good, that he's able to appreciate the beauty around him ... if I *am* beautiful, which, you know, I guess everyone hopes they *are*, to some extent, but it's not something I've obsessed about all that much. I'm more focused on the thought processes, the personality traits, the workings of the brain and so on—and where was I going with this?

He thinks I'm beautiful.

And then his hand eases around the nape of my neck and he doesn't just kiss me, but licks at my lips and pushes his tongue into my mouth, thrusting softly between kisses.

Oh my god.

I don't even know how to do this!

This isn't the kiss of a fresh-faced, restrained boy scout.

This is the kiss of a lusty alpha male who has lived hard and known darkness and who is *very* good at this.

I let him taste me and kiss me, mostly because it's the most erotic thing that's ever happened to me and also because I have no choice. He's *aggressive*. And unbelievably strong. His muscles are all coiled and huge. His other arm slides around me, holding me in place, and his grip is ridiculous. He could obviously overpower me if he wanted to—*and I think he might*—with very little effort at all. He almost seems like he might lose control any second and it's a little bit scary but is also making me hot … *and wet. Oh god.*

If I want him to stop, I need to tell him right now. If we take this any further than a scorching kiss, he might not be *able* to stop, I can feel this. His energy is controlled, but barely, like a flood is being held back by a precarious wall and is about to break loose in a torrential flood of feeling and need.

There's no going slow, I can sense that. It's all or nothing. If I try to push him away now, he'll cage that energy. He'll retreat into his cave of emotion and shut himself off from me.

I don't want him to do that.

I want to *feel* him. Because the things he's doing are awakening a piece of myself I've been curious about but have never been able to allow or indulge. Until now.

I want to unleash his raging need. I want to find out what that *feels* like.

Are you sure about that, Violet? some inner voice is saying. *You have no idea what you're getting yourself into here.*

I don't even know him. I should wait until our third or fourth date, if this even *is* a date, like you're supposed to. I should slow this down and not jump the gun here. It's happening too fast.

Then again, I'll turn nineteen in less than three months and I've never really even been touched. Which is no way to live, come to think of it.

I want to live a little.

Or a lot.

If I'm going to have a one night stand, it might as well be with an ultra-hot combat soldier. Bo told Millie—who told me—that Caleb got awarded a medal of honor for saving two men's lives. He's a war hero. And he's sexy as hell.

So what if I hardly know him.

Lust is winning over reason or prudence, which I'm sick to death of.

I want him. I want to accept his challenge and issue one of my own. He's so damn gorgeous. My body feels loose-limbed and lust-drunk with his effect as his tongue thrusts deep. I give him my tongue and he starts sucking lightly and I make a little noise because when he sucks on my tongue, it sends shooting currents of pleasure to the low pit of my stomach, and lower, where I'm getting warm and tingly.

I fully realize that in this moment I'm making a choice.

I can tell he likes the little noise I made because he

makes one too, something between a savage sigh and a growl-edged purr.

"Violet," he whispers gruffly. "Do you want this? Because you are so fucking beautiful. I want you so much."

"Yes." I'm a little scared. *He's so big.* So ludicrously strong.

I guess that was all the invitation he needed because he's pulling my dress over my head. He tosses it aside. "You sure?" he asks, but he doesn't even wait for me to answer. We're too far gone to stop.

He pulls the string on my bikini top and it falls away. *Oh my god.* My breasts feel full and soft in the warm air. Caleb's hands cup my breasts and he covers my nipple with his hot mouth, sucking and swirling it with his tongue. "Fuck, you're so damn sweet," he murmurs against my skin. His fingers find my other nipple and he squeezes and plays it until both my nipples feel painfully hard and sensitive. Caleb deepens the lusty pulls of his mouth, licking and sucking like he's feeding from my breasts as he grips me with bruising fingers. Each pull of his mouth makes my pussy feel softer. *And wetter.* My bikini is clinging damply and the warmth is turning into deep, sweet throbs that are threatening to overflow.

Oh god. This is intense.

He's rough and he's dirty. "I'm so fucking hard for you, baby, I'm losing my mind. I've been dreaming about you. I can't stop thinking about you. Since that very first second, when I saw you by the pool. I couldn't fucking believe my eyes."

He's fighting to keep his control. I can feel the effort he's making as he barely loosens his grip on me, like he realizes he's leaving marks.

I don't want him to pull back. The thing is … I wonder if I can make him … *lose* control. I have this feeling I can … very easily.

His effect is making me feel reckless and … *hungry.*

I want to. With him. Right now.

I've never done this before, but I'm pretty sure I know how to start.

I'm in college now, I'm young and free and I have never in my life met a more physically beautiful human being in my life as Caleb McCabe. I've never felt as good as he's making me feel right now.

I have this urge not to waste time.

And so do I.

The moon is overhead, almost full, and when I look down at Caleb's jeans I can see his … *holy hell!* It's freaking *huge.* His top button is undone and his cock is halfway out the waistband of his jeans. It's hot-looking and the head is shiny with moisture.

Caleb is still kissing and sucking my nipples.

What he's doing to me is kind of making me feel like I'm on fire with lust, and I want to … touch him. I reach down and slide my fingertips across the wetness on the tip of his cock. Gently, I swirl it around. A gush of liquid comes out and his cock gets all slippery.

I hear a low oath. "If you keep doing that, honey, I'm going to come all over you, and I don't want to do that until I've tasted your sweet pussy and made you come with my tongue."

Oh my god.

I guess I've figured out how to get Caleb McCabe to talk.

He lays me back on the couch-like seats, so I'm lying flat. Caleb moves down my body. He's kissing my stomach, licking the tiny butterfly tattoo on my hip. "I love it," he murmurs. Then I feel a light tug and—*oh*—he just *ripped off* my bikini bottom.

I *have* made him lose control and it's almost scary. It feels dangerous.

When he sees I'm completely bare, he groans. I decided to get totally waxed just for fun when I first went away to school. Part of my whole I'm-wild-and-away-from-home freedom kick. Caleb seems spellbound by the sight for a few seconds. "Holy fuck," he whispers. Then he kind of goes a little crazy. He pushes my legs apart and starts kissing and greedily eating at my pussy. His tongue licks me open. I moan and squirm because it's so intense and intimate, but his grip is too strong. He won't even let me move.

Even if I wanted to get away from him now, I really don't think he'd let me go. There's an edge to his passion, like it's stronger than he is.

The warm glide of his tongue feels so warm and *so freaking good*, my body goes loose and submissive.

My hand finds the hard muscle of his upper arm, where I can feel the brutal power of him. The sheer size and raw strength of him are stunningly arousing. I'm at his mercy. *And I want to be.* He pushes my legs so they're bent and apart and I let him—not that I have a choice. His greedy tongue thrusts inside me. He circles my clit, playing it. Then his hungry mouth latches on to me. His fingers ease their way inside me, rubbing and coaxing. The light throb explodes into something else altogether. The pleasure crashes through me in furtive bursts. I'm writhing against his mouth. He holds me there, feasting on me like he's starving.

"That's it, baby," he murmurs. "Come for me. You taste like heaven."

My orgasm is still happening. There's weight on top of me and I realize he's above me now, sliding his hard, slippery cock against my thigh. *Oh god.* He's pressing himself against my still-rippling core. He's rubbing me with his thick length and it feels *so unbelievably good*. My pussy is cradling his cock, pulsing around him like my body is inviting him inside.

As the broad head of his cock forces its way inside me, I gasp in a whisper, "I'm on the pill." Also part of my new freedom kick. Not that he seems particularly concerned either way.

Caleb makes a sound, like he might be glad about that, but he's already partly inside me.

He's so freaking *big*. It *hurts…* but his fingers are skating back and forth over my clit and—*it's happening again* —his other fingers are doing the same thing to the intimate cove of my ass, which shocks me beyond belief, but I hear myself moaning his name. *Caleb. Oh god, Caleb, I'm coming.*

Is this normal? To have it happen like this your very first time? Somewhere beyond the haze of my rush, I realize it probably isn't normal. Nothing about Caleb McCabe is normal. I'm glad. I like him like this. Wild. Complicated. Unrelenting. *Addictive.*

He's biting my neck, growling, gripping me, pushing his way deeper inside me. "You feel so fucking good, Violet. I'm going to make you come so hard, baby."

He is. My ecstasy spins out into longer, deeper ripples. Caleb is *riding* those ripples. With each clench of my tender flesh around him, his thick cock slides deeper. There's pain, but *I'm still coming.* His fingers won't let me *stop* coming. They slide and swirl as his big cock stretches me and possesses me completely. I'm so *full* of him. He's so very big and deep and thick inside me, sliding and rearing against every sweet spot I never even knew I had.

"*Fuck,*" he groans. "I can't hold this, honey, you feel too good. Are you ready for me?"

He thrusts deeply and I cry out because it hurts but I'm coming even harder. It's too much. My inner muscles clench tightly around his slick, massive bulk until his cock starts throbbing hotly as he growls. I can feel the flooding bursts of his warm cum filling me as the tight tugs of my body milk him over and over.

It lasts a long time.

I'm floating on some kind of blissed-out cloud.

Caleb's breathing is heavy. He exhales a low, disbelieving sigh. He's holding his weight so he won't crush me. His barely-softened big cock is still thickly wedged deep inside me. My legs are wrapped around his waist, my knees fully bent. He's heavy and possessive. He won't let me move. It's like I'm his now. He kisses me, pushing his tongue into my mouth. Then he stares dreamily into my eyes and I hardly recognize him. That haunted look is, for the moment, completely gone.

I did that. And I want to keep him here, with me and nowhere else.

"Violet," he says, his voice deep and gravel-edged. "Holy hell, you're so *gorgeous*. I've never come that hard in my life."

Me either, I want to say, but I can't even speak. I'm overcome with an ocean of vast, deep emotion.

"I want to stay right here, just like this, forever," he says, his voice husky.

"Okay," I whisper.

"This is the best thing that's ever happened to me. I know what that sounds like, but it is. This. Right here. Right now. You."

We stay like that for a long time and he kisses me and

gazes at me and it's really the most connective, intimate thing.

"I love how you feel," he murmurs, kissing me again. He's romantic, which sort of surprises me. "I love your hair and your eyes and your lips. I love everything."

Okay, wow.

I touch his thick hair and I kiss him back, opening to him. I suck gently on his tongue. I can feel that he's lengthening inside me, getting fully hard again, already. I almost want to say, *I can't. It's too much.* But Caleb thrusts into me and my soreness only makes the full thickness of his cock feel *good.* Unbelievably good. The pain is pleasure-heavy, building into a dark, sweet ache.

"God, you drive me crazy," he growls. "Can you feel how hard you make me? Can you feel how much I want you?"

He holds me down with his weight. He's so deep inside me. So hard and thick and slick. Forcing the pleasure even deeper with his big, driving body. I can't take it. It's too much. I moan with a pain and pleasure so rich with feeling, my whole body starts coming. I moan and squirm just to try to *deal* with the brimming, squeezing overload. Caleb groans as his thick cock jerks violently inside me, flooding me again with his silky heat, and the pulse of it spins my orgasm over another edge, shattering me all over again. Wave after wave of it. A vast, star-bursting ocean of pleasure.

Eventually, I resurface. I'm totally spent. I can't even move.

"*Caleb*," I murmur.

He kisses my face and murmurs lust words and love words in my ear. *I love being inside you. Everything about you is so damn beautiful I can hardly stand it.*

We lay there for a while. Kissing. Touching. Staring into each other's eyes, so fully in the moment, like we can't believe how *good* this is. How real. We're divinely, fully connected.

Caleb McCabe has somehow changed everything.

I hold him even tighter. I don't want this to end. I want to keep him here, all to myself.

His body gets heavier. I like how heavy he is. How big he is inside me. He moves us so he's not crushing me, keeping himself inside. With the movement, I can feel his seed over-flowing, dripping down my thighs.

Wow.

I've given myself to him. I've had sex with Caleb McCabe.

I'm still *having sex with Caleb McCabe.*

Something about this feels, in this moment, perfect. It feels right. I can't explain it, but it does.

My eyes close.

I don't know if I've ever felt as content and connected and emotional and alive as I do right now, with him, under the starry violet sky.

8

CALEB

I'M IN HEAVEN. Nothing has ever felt this good.

Her softness. Her warmth. Her sweet perfection. She feels astoundingly good.

The whispers begin at the back of my mind, like creeping tendrils of thick smoke.

I shouldn't be here. I was never supposed to be here.

Look what I've done.

Look what I've done to her.

The lush beauty of her overwhelms my senses. I pull away. I'm aware of a gush of liquid as I leave her. Ours. Mine, mostly. It breaks my heart.

Above me, white clouds turn black. Blue sky goes dark.

I'm cold but I'm burning.

I miss her.

But heaven is no place for someone like me. I killed them all. I couldn't save the ones who needed me. My hands are covered in blood.

I need to wash them.

I don't want any of it to get onto her. *The angel can't be touched.*

It will kill me if I taint her with my sins and my downfall.

But I already have.

I jerk away, and I fall onto a hard surface. I reach for the railing and pull myself up.

I can hear their voices.

Come on, man. Who'd have thought we'd get in? he jokes. It's bright. Come with us.

Logan's voice.

Did you give my mother what was left of me?

And Quinn's.

The shadows want me back. They grab at my ankles where the flames burn me. They're as sticky as tar.

They'll take me if I don't fight.

Even worse, they'll take her. *They'll drag her under right along with me.*

Everything I touch turns to blood and pain and dust.

I pull myself over the railing and I jump.

The water is jarringly cold and blissfully quiet. I drift. I could just let myself go. The mad, fiery shadows would never find me here.

Caleb.

Caleb.

It's her. She's calling to me.

If only I could stay with her. If only I deserved her.

If only I wasn't already doomed.

CALEB.

All right. I'll see what she wants.

I break the surface and—fuck.

I'm in the water. My lungs burn as I gasp deep breaths of air.

"Caleb!"

I look up and she's there.

Fuck, she's beautiful.

"Caleb, climb up! Climb up the ladder. *Please*. Do it now."

I can see the chrome rungs attached to the side of the boat.

"Caleb, please climb up! Or I'm coming in. Climb up! Right now."

I don't want her coming in. It's cold. I want her safe. And warm.

And as far away from me and the black, swallowing darkness that will only end up consuming us both.

"*Caleb.* All right, that's it. I'm coming in."

"No." I grab the lowest rung and I start climbing up. I get to the top, with effort, and I jump over the railing. She hugs me, even though I'm cold and wet.

"*Jesus*, Caleb. You scared me."

She's crying. She's so small. So perfect. She looks up at me with heart-breaking eyes. "You're going to be okay, Caleb. Everything's okay."

I wipe her tears with my thumbs.

If only that was true.

9

Violet

SOMETHING WAKES me and my eyes open.

We must have dozed off for a while. Caleb's grip is even stronger than before—too strong. He's hurting me. His whole body is unbelievably tense and hard.

He lifts his weight from me and he slides from my body and *I don't want him to leave me*. I feel ridiculously emotional about this, like I *need* him. Like he's taken a piece of myself with him.

I'm crying, weirdly. Warm tears slide down my face.

Something's wrong.

Caleb rolls away from me and falls to the deck. Hard.

He seems out of it. He grabs the railing and pulls himself up.

And he jumps over the side of the boat.

What the—? "Caleb!"

What's he *doing?*

And then I realize. *He's having a nightmare.* He's in the grip of some kind of hallucination and *he's in the water.*

"*Caleb!*"

I run to the railing and scream his name.

But he's still under.

Oh my god. He's drowning!

I scream his name again.

I find a life jacket and I'm about to jump in when he surfaces.

His eyes are still clouded with his nightmare. "Caleb. Climb up! Climb up the ladder. *Please.* Do it now." After more pleading, he finally does.

As soon as he's back on deck, I wrap my arms around his big, muscular body. He's cold.

Physically cold and … emotionally cold.

Something in him has changed.

I want *my* Caleb back. The dreamy Caleb who gazed at me and said all those sweet words. This Caleb feels a million miles from sweetness.

He pulls away, and goes over to the cushioned couch, which was our bed only a few minutes ago, where a white towel is still draped. He grabs it and as he does, he freezes in place as he notices in the bright moonlight a red stain on the terrycloth.

He stares at it for a few seconds, then his stony gaze slides to me. To my body. To my thighs. I look down to see what he's staring at and I see it too.

Blood. Streaked across my upper thigh.

"Violet?" His voice sounds alarmed. More than that. Appalled. Absolutely agonized. He touches his fingers to my skin. "Holy *fuck*, Violet."

"It's o-okay," I stammer. I'm not used to this level of intimacy with another person. Especially one who suddenly seems so furious. "It was … it was my first ti—"

"You're a fucking *virgin*? Why didn't you *tell* me that?"

God. He doesn't have be so aggressive about it, nightmare or no nightmare. "Why does it matter?"

"Why does it *matter*? It matters! I *hurt* you."

"You didn't *hurt* me. I wanted to—"

"I *did*. You're *bleeding*."

"*You* didn't do that. I mean, the blood's just—"

"I know what the blood *means*, Violet. For fuck's sake! You should have *told* me." He runs a hand through his hair, like he's about to lose his grip. He's not breathing well. God, he looks so tough. And mean. *And so beautiful.* "You're crying."

I don't entirely understand his reaction. Why is he so upset? More tears paint warm lines down my face. I don't even know why I'm crying. Maybe because he's being a bastard all of a sudden. Something in him has flipped. I miss what we had for a brief moment in time and I want it back. His nightmare and the whole jumping-into-the-water-and-nearly-drowning thing was crazy and unnerving. And now this rash fury that I'm really not sure how to deal with.

"I'm not crying," I say lamely. I am, but not for the reasons he thinks. I wipe my tears away impatiently.

"You are. And it's my fucking fault." I don't think I've ever seen anyone look more tormented than Caleb does right now, like the weight of the world is more than he can bear.

"I'm *okay*, Caleb." I reach up to touch his face but he flinches and I can't stop more tears from leaking out of my eyes because I don't want him to feel the way he feels right now. He's got it all wrong. "You didn't *hurt* me, Caleb. I'm crying because you scared me when you jumped overboard. And because you just blew my mind in the best possible way. I *wanted* you to do what you did. All of it. Everything."

He doesn't seem to be hearing me. He gets a bottle of water and a towel. "Here," he says gruffly. "Sit down. Lay back."

I do, because I'll give him anything. I want to get back to that place we were before.

Very, very gently, he cleans away the blood and the stickiness of our lovemaking. Then he sits me up and drapes a blanket around my shoulders, carefully wrapping it around me. He dries himself and pulls on his jeans.

He goes inside the front room, where the controls of the boat are located. I follow him. I've been on enough boats to know the sound of an electric anchor being lifted.

"Why are you bringing up the anchor?"

"We're going back."

"I don't want to go back yet. I want to stay here a little longer."

"No." The way he says it is abrupt and emotionless.

"Why not? Caleb. I don't understand why you're—"

"I said we're going back."

I try not to feel hurt by what he's doing. I know it's not his fault, but still. He hasn't just changed, he's completely transformed. From beautiful lover into cold, emotionless jerk. I try to be patient with him, and imagine what's going through his head. I grasp to find something to relate to in the way he's acting. "Caleb, I know you had a nightmare. I've read about—"

He pins me with a scathing glare.

Maybe it's not time to bring up the list of symptoms I've been studying in Psych 101. "Can we at least talk about what just happened?"

His tone is flat. "I don't want to talk about it. What I want to do is take you back to shore and let you get on with your life, as far away from me as possible."

"Caleb. *No.* I don't want you to do that."

"It's best this way, trust me."

"No. It isn't best." *Goddamn it.* I'm crying again. "I know you've been through some terrible things. I understand that. I want to help—"

"You can't. And I refuse to drag you down with me." His knuckles are white where he's clutching the steering wheel. He glances over at me. Somewhere behind the pain and the shut-down blankness of his expression, there's a brief, passing hint of the heat and tenderness of what we shared, like a blue glow behind his eyes. "Violet. You're a goddamn *angel*. But what happened tonight was a mistake."

I'm crying harder now, even though I'm trying not to. "How can you say that?"

"I wish I'd never met you. I wish I'd never touched you. It shouldn't have happened."

The cold, measured *mean*ness of his words is doing more than upsetting me. It's making me angry. I want to rile him. I want to shake him out of this. "Well, I'm *glad* you touched me. I'm glad you fucked me."

I think we're both taken aback by what I've just said. "Violet—"

But I don't care. Something in me has crossed over. "I am. I'm glad you took my virginity and made me bleed."

He levels his gaze at me. He's shocked by my words, and so am I. But I want him to be shocked. I want to dig deeper.

"And I'm glad you came inside me. It felt good. More than good. It made me come, over and over. I can still feel you there."

Caleb stands over me, sort of looming. If I didn't know better, I'd feel threatened by his size and his fury. "Well, you need to *forget* what it feels like. Because it's never going to happen again. It was a mistake and it's over."

"But *why*? Why are you being like this? I don't *want* it to be over!"

He doesn't answer me. His concentration shifts to the mooring of the boat. We're back at the dock.

He kills the engine and goes to tie up the boat. Then he comes over to me and, with that same hard coldness, he lifts me into his arms.

"Put me down! Just leave here, then. I'm staying on the boat."

I struggle but it's like struggling against a vice grip. "No. I'm taking you up to the house."

Being this close to him again, feeling the extreme warmth and strength of him, breathing in that heady scent of raw masculinity and the musk of hot sex makes me realize what's at stake here. What just happened was unexpected, too fast and reckless as hell, but I don't care. I think, already and despite everything, I might be half in love with him. I'm worried about his state of mind. And I don't want to let him go. Not yet.

Caleb starts carrying me, wrapped in the blanket (my bikini is long gone and I have no idea where my dress is), up a trail that leads to the lake house. I've only seen it from a distance. Compared to the main house, it's smaller and more modern-looking.

I want to tell him I don't understand what he's doing or why he's doing it. But of course I *do* understand it. This is my test. This is the part where I need to try to figure out how I can get through to some of what's caused his trauma. To gently dig it out and allow it to breathe. Only then will he be able to start letting some of it go. But how?

We get to the door, which he opens. He takes me inside

and places me gently on a large couch that faces a wall of windows and the view.

It's dark in here, but there's enough light from the moon to shed a soft glow over the interior space. The house is made of glass and stone and pale wood. It's luxurious in an understated kind of way. You can tell at just a glance that it's incredibly well-designed.

Caleb disappears, then returns with a duvet, which he tucks around me. He places a phone on the coffee table next to me. He goes to the open plan kitchen and gets a glass of water which he sets next to the phone.

"Come sit with me." If I can get him to sit with me, I can … I don't know. Convince him. Change his mind. "Caleb, I know it feels like you'll never get over the things that happened to you. But you will. You can. It'll get better, I promise. Please. Sit here with me."

"No. I'm leaving." He picks up a sweatshirt that was draped over a chair and he pulls it on.

Leaving? "Where are you going? Up to the other house? I'll come with you."

"My brother Gage lives in Chicago. I told him I'd visit as soon as I got home."

I start to get up. "But … now?"

"I'm sorry, Violet." He walks over to the couch and crouches down in front of me. The blanket that's wound around me falls off my shoulder, which he stares at like he's mesmerized, but then he looks into my eyes and takes my cool hand in his much warmer one. "I'm sorry I hurt you. I should have stopped myself but I couldn't. You felt too fucking good. But that doesn't change the fact that I never should have touched you. I'm leaving. It's the only way I can stop myself from hurting you again. It has to be this way."

The damn tears won't stop pooling. "But I don't *want* you to leave. I already told you, I *wanted* you to do everything you did. It was beautiful. You know it was. You can't change that. You can't … *rewrite* how amazing it was. Please. Please stay."

God, he looks anguished. His eyes are a darker, duller shade of blue, as though a light has gone out behind them. "I can't be with you. I'm really fucked up. I think I'll always be fucked up. Whatever we might have had … it'll never end well. Because of me. And I refuse to put you through that." I can tell by his eyes and his voice that he's completely shut himself off from me. "It *was* beautiful. I meant it when I said it was the most beautiful thing that's ever happened to me. But it can't *continue* to be beautiful. I'll only end up ruining your life. I'm leaving, before I can inflict any more damage."

"Caleb, I don't care about that. I want you to—"

"Please don't try to talk me out of it."

I stare into his unfathomable eyes and I can see there that he's not going to budge. "Can you at least wait until morning?"

"If I do that, I'll never leave. And I have to go."

"But I don't want you to." Tears leak from my eyes hotly.

He leans in slowly and very, very gently, he kisses my mouth. "You are insanely beautiful. Everything about you. Which is why I can't do this to you." He lets go of my hand and clenches his own hand into a fist. "Forget about me and get on with your life."

"Caleb," I sob. I try to think of the right thing to say. "Please stay. Please don't go."

But he's already walking out the door.

10

CALEB

I'M DOING over a hundred miles an hour on my Ducati and I don't give a fuck. If I crash and the world ends, at least I won't have to *feel* anymore.

Her tears.

Her blood.

Why hadn't she *told* me she was a *fucking virgin?* Jesus Christ. I took her like a goddamn maniac, like there was no tomorrow. For *hours.* Hell, if given the chance I'd live inside that girl until the end of time.

Her body.

The way she felt when she was coming. That tight little squeezing pussy, driving me to insanity. That look in her eyes, like I was worthy of her.

I can't take this.

It would have *hurt*. I'm big and rough and heavy and she's … perfect.

She didn't even say anything. Or maybe she did. Maybe those little whimpers she was making weren't about pleasure, but about pain.

Maybe I'm so out of practice I can't even fucking tell.

I forced myself on her, spending myself inside her more than once—did she whisper something about being on the pill or did I dream that? I didn't care. I don't know *why* I didn't care, but it didn't even enter my mind. Which is crazy, especially considering the fact that I've never had sex without a condom in my life.

And then what? I stormed away and told her I didn't want to talk about it.

Nice.

What a fucking knight in goddamn shining armor.

But it has to be this way. I'm the very last thing that girl needs in her life. You couldn't find a more dazzling woman if you scoured the earth for the rest of your life. And what do I do at my very first opportunity? Dirty her. Take out all my frustrations on that sweet, flawless slice of heaven, leaving her crying and bloody. Taking her virginity … so *aggressively*.

Did she even want *me to?*

Am I so far gone that I thought she wanted it when maybe … she didn't?

I can't be. She kissed me so sweetly. *Her mouth. Goddamn*

it. Those weren't the kisses of a girl who was protesting …
were they?

My brain feels like it's been demolished. I don't know how to read things anymore. I don't know how to be normal or *feel* in a normal way.

Which is why I need to put distance between myself and my new obsession.

I'm going 140 now. It's dawn and the landscape blurs. I could veer off the road, and it would all be over. The pain would feel good. It would be quick, and my mind could finally be quiet. Peaceful. Whatever that means.

I think of Logan, like I always do when I feel close to the edge. The joking prankster who seemed untouchable and larger than life. Turns out, he wasn't. I can almost hear him scolding me from all the way over there in the afterlife. *You fucking pussy! Don't you dare opt out, man. Live! Give it everything you've got while you still can.*

I slow down a little. To 120.

I'm going insane, that's all there is to it.

I get to Chicago and drive through the city. It's the very beginning of rush hour. I weave in and out of traffic. A few people honk at me and give me the finger but I really couldn't care less. I park in front of my brother's building, which he owns. His offices are in the lower floors and he lives in the top floor apartment, with a view to the lake. He's done well for himself, even if he did have to trample his way over a lot of people to get there. Gage is ruthless and possibly one of the biggest pricks on planet Earth. He's also the one person in the world who might—just *might*—be able to help me. Bo is the more empathetic of my brothers, and is a good person to talk to, but he's clearly so distracted and whipped by his new girlfriend he can barely see straight.

I need the no-nonsense, bullshit-free advice of my older brother, who's without a doubt the most cynical mother-fucker I know.

He's just arriving at his office and as soon as he sees me, I can tell from his expression that I look like shit.

"Holy fuck," Gage says, giving me a critical once-over before hugging me. "You look like hell."

"Not surprising, since I also feel like hell."

He steps back and gives me another once-over. "When did you get so fucking *buff*? Jesus. Get in here." He pulls me into the elevator, which takes us ten floors up. We come to a stop and the door slides open. To his assistant, he barks, "Cancel everything I have today. This is my brother, the goddamn war hero. I haven't seen him in more than a year." Then he shuts the door behind us.

His views are spectacular. They're the kind of views that announce to everyone who walks into this room that Gage McCabe is a hotshot. And a very rich one. "When did you get back? And what are you doing here? I told you I was coming home this weekend."

"I needed to clear my head."

"By driving four hours in the middle of the night?"

I stare at him for a second. I don't tell him it actually took less than three hours to make the trip since I drove like a bat out of hell the whole way. Gage's hair is a shade darker than mine, almost black, and his eyes are a lighter shade of blue. An almost royal blue, like our father's. He's been working out since I saw him last. He looks a lot burlier.

"Fuck, man. Let me see where you got cut open." He sits in his chair and motions for me to sit on his couch, but I don't.

I lift up my sweatshirt—all I'm wearing is a sweatshirt, jeans, a pair of combat boots and a leather jacket—and I show him my scars, which are still red in places but don't really hurt anymore.

"Shit."

"The shrapnel missed all my major organs. According to my doctors, I'm very lucky."

His eyes narrow. "What's the bruise on your neck? If I didn't know better I'd say that was a hickey. What are we doing, dating a teenager?"

Hell. She probably *is* a teenager. She's a freshman. She's probably eighteen or nineteen. And what did I do to all that innocent beauty? *Used* her, pumped her full of my hot cum, more than once, then left her in the dust.

Is she okay? What's she doing right now? Still crying? Still … bleeding?

Gage reads my silence. "You *are* dating a teenager?" My brother is smart and perceptive as fuck. It's impossible to hide things from him. He sits back in his chair and folds his arms. He's watching my face, searching for clues. "You've only been back in the country for a week. I talked to Bo a day and a half ago. He said you walked in the door, went straight to bed and stayed there for six days. So you somehow managed to charm a teenager, get laid, then drive to Chicago, all in a matter of … twelve hours? Nicely done."

I can't take this. Because I *miss* her so much it literally hurts. I'm having another one of those mini heart attacks. The pain is worse than any flying shrapnel. I'm craving her so hard, the memory of her is ripping at the edges of my sanity.

The way she tasted, like the sweetest honey.

Goddamn it!

I left her there, alone and crying.

What if she goes to someone else for comfort after my asshole behavior … *like Hayes?* In a sudden fit of rage, I punch the wall, making a huge dent in the drywall.

Gage stands up and walks over to me. He slings his arm around my shoulders and starts steering me toward the door. "Okay. I knew we'd have issues, but I clearly underestimated the extent of it. We're going to get some food, possibly a shot or two of whiskey to calm your nerves, and we're going to start to talk about whatever the fuck it is you're dealing with."

I thought it might help to talk some of this out, but now I just feel pissed off. And so fucking sad.

But Gage is right. The first two shots of whiskey take the edge off.

We're at some dimly-lit, upmarket bar & grill. We're

sitting in a booth by the front window that's secluded from the other tables. "Right," he says. "First things first. Who's the teenager?"

I could keep the details from him but what's the point? Gage has a way of prying things out of me, for better or for worse. He'll keep ordering shots until I tell him everything. "Her name is Violet Aurora Jameson."

Gage is glaring at me with measured concern, like something about the way I've said her name or that I even *know* her name is troubling.

"She's Bo's girlfriend's roommate."

"Is this the one Bo is gaga all over and is bringing perfectly good football games to a standstill to stare at? What's her name again?"

"Millie. And yeah, Bo's a goner."

"*Fuck.*" Unlike Bo, Gage doesn't have a romantic bone in his body. "Either way, it was about time that kid got laid. No wonder he's obsessed. He finally figured out what he's been missing out on. His 'promise' was ridiculous." Gage is the last person on earth who would self-impose celibacy.

The waitress arrives to take our food orders. "Hi, Gage," she smiles at him. "You said you'd call me last week."

"Did I?"

Her gaze lands on me. "Who's this?"

"My brother, who's strictly off limits." Gage flirts, charms-in-a-playboy/asshole-kind-of-way and then beds most of the women he meets. It's nothing new. "Bring us another round."

"It's nine o'clock in the fucking morning, Gage," I tell him, after the waitress walks away. "I have enough problems."

"Consider it therapy. I'll make sure we get home safe. It'll loosen you up."

Who knows, maybe it'll help. Nothing else is, so I may as well go with it.

"So you got laid last night. What's the big deal? Why are you punching holes in walls over it?"

I can't think of a way to begin to answer that. So I start with, "She's a freshman."

He exhales a laugh. "Shit."

"Yeah. I first met her the day I got back. By the pool. I was too shell-shocked to even speak to her. I just stood there like a fucking idiot."

"Understandable," Gage says, and I'm thankful that he *gets* me on some level. "You just got back from *war*, bud. It's okay to take time to adjust."

"I guess so. Anyway, Bo had a party yesterday. She was there. I needed some air. I decided to take the boat out. She came along for a ride."

"Let me guess. And one thing led to another …"

One thing led to the most beautiful and intense night of my goddamn life. She felt like nothing else on this earth. And this is going to sound cheesy as hell, but it felt real. *It felt like the real fucking thing.*

The waitress arrives with two more shots, scolds Gage again coyly for not calling her, then disappears. I throw mine back and Gage does the same.

Maybe it's the whiskey. I hear myself confessing. "I had a flashback last night. A bad one. We were still on the boat. I woke up in the water."

"In the *water*? Fuck. What happened?"

I almost let myself go. I almost fucking did it. But she called me back. There she was, crying and dirtied by my rampaging lust. "I woke up. I climbed back onto the boat. I took her home. And then I left."

"Nothing wrong with leaving after the fact. I do it all the time."

"I can't do relationships. Not now. Maybe I'll never be capable of it."

"So? Just have sex with her every now and then. Get her out of your system, and when you've had enough, send her some flowers, tell her it was fun and move on."

I consider not even telling Gage, because I'm not sure he gets where I'm going with this. He's a player who thinks monogamy is a dirty word. But I'm three shots in and I just blurt it out anyway. "I can't."

"You can't what? I thought you said you already did."

"I can't 'just' have sex with Violet. It won't be enough. There's nothing casual about the way I feel."

"You've known her for *a day*, bro."

"And a night," I point out.

Gage stares at me. "Jesus Christ. First Bo and now you? Is there something in the water up there? Maybe I won't come home this weekend after all. I don't want to get infected."

I ignore this.

"Well, then," he says, "if you're as into her as you seem to think you are, my advice would be to take her out again and see where it goes. Maybe the whole 'nothing casual about the way I feel' sentiment will fade once you spend more time with her. That's what usually—who am I kidding—that's what *always* happens to me."

"I can't take her out again, that's the problem."

"Why not?"

"Because." This is hard to talk about. "I'm capable of …"

"Of … ?" He's waiting for me to finish.

It takes me a few seconds to say the word, and if it wasn't for the whiskey, I don't think I could go there. "Violence. I'm fucked up, Gage. I'm dangerous. I'm unpredictable. I have nightmares every night and they make me scream and sweat and do things I'm not in control of."

"That's not *you*. That's your trauma. "

"Whatever. It's all the same thing."

Gage contemplates me. He doesn't ask for intimate details, which is good, because I'm not about to give any. "Did *she* say that? That you did something violent?"

Stay. Please don't leave. You can't rewrite how amazing it was. Please stay.

I sigh and run my hand along the stubble of my jaw. "No. I don't know. But it could happen."

He's quiet for a while, and when he continues, his tone is more serious. "Caleb," he says. Which sounds strange. He usually calls me "dude" or "bud" or "bro" or "idiot" or "C.J.," my childhood nickname, since my middle name is John, so hearing him say my name like that has impact. "You just spent a year in a war zone, man. You were doing your job in an extremely dangerous situation. You're a highly trained professional who was acting in the line of duty. You earned a purple heart, for fuck's sake. You're good at your job. Taken out of that context, though, I'm a hundred percent sure you're incapable of any kind of violence whatsoever against someone you care about."

I'm taken off-guard by what he says. But I'm not convinced. "You can't know that. I don't trust myself anymore." *She was crying. She was bleeding.*

"I've known you longer than anyone," Gage says, "and I *do* know that. I'd bet my life on it. You were always the kid who went out of his way to help people. The kid who refused to kill a spider and instead would take it outside and make a little house for it out of leaves. You're a badass, Caleb, and you're buff as fuck—I mean, Jesus, *look* at you. There's no doubt you *could* do damage if you wanted to. But you won't. Because at your deepest level you're *kind*. The kindest person I know. And the most honorable, decent and *good*. Not like your asshole of a big brother. You'll treat that girl like a princess, even in the middle of your deepest, darkest flashbacks. It's just the way you are."

I glare at my brother. Neither of us says anything for a few seconds. I really, really want to believe he's right. "You think so?"

"I know so. If you want to have an actual relationship with this girl and see where it leads, tell her that. Tell her your concerns. Track her down, kiss the hell out of her, get some fucking therapy, tell her how you feel and see what she says. You definitely don't lack courage, C.J., at least not when it comes to war or football. What have you got to lose?"

"I don't know." My heart?

"Listen," Gage says, "I'm the last person in the world who should be doling out advice along these lines, but you of all people should know that life is short. Have a good time while you still can. Look at what happened to Mom and Dad, and your brothers in arms who didn't make it. Fucking go for it, if that's really how you feel."

The waitress brings our breakfasts and two beers along with two more shots and we clink them together. "To the people we've lost," Gage says.

Gage and I get fucking hammered. We go up to his apartment and drink some wine and listen to music and talk for the rest of the day. We talk about our parents, and the heaviness of the loss, something we've never really done. We're far enough away now from the freshness of the grief that we can talk about it more openly, maybe.

I tell him a few details about my time in Afghanistan. Not everything, but I tell him as much as I can handle. I don't mention Logan, but he asks about the purple heart and I tell him the abridged version of the story. Talking feels like letting it out, and once it's out, some of it actually feels like it *stays* out, like I've let go of a small corner of the angst and now it's just … gone.

We pass out at some point in the evening and, amazingly, I don't have any nightmares at all.

I dream of her. Her smile and her freckles and that long, red-gold hair that's as soft as feathers.

When I wake up, I feel a little better.

I know without a doubt that I will not be needing another drink for a very long time.

And I've made my decision. I can only hope Gage is right.

This is a different kind of fear than worrying about getting shot or aiming too far to the left.

This fear has to do with taking a different kind of risk. She might not forgive me for what I've already done. She might turn me down. Or I might disappoint her, or drive her away with all my demons.

But, fuck it. I'd rather *try* than spend the rest of my life pining for the one that got away. The one who, somehow, has already filled up all the space in my head and my heart. And other parts of me.

So I shake my brother's hand, which turns into a man-hug. "I'll be up on the weekend," he says, "but I'm bringing my own water."

I jump back on my Ducati and I head toward home, with one thing on my mind.

Her.

11

I CAN'T BELIEVE what an *asshole* he is!

Caleb McCabe is an uncaring, selfish, brutish jerk.

And also a beautiful, hot, huge, unbelievably-good-at-that, sex-on-a-stick dream.

I don't know what to do.

He left me.

He made love to me—that's absolutely what it felt like—and then he walked away.

How could he *do* that?

I want him.

My body feels hyper-awake, still riding the high of my lingering endorphin rush. I'm aware of all my new sorenesses. *I've been used.* No. I've been *enlightened.* Now I know what all the fuss is about.

I wish there was someone I could talk to. But it's five

thirty in the morning and Millie is most definitely in bed with Bo. I'm hardly going to knock on their bedroom door and give them both a play by play of how I lost my virginity to his brother.

My own brothers would freak if I called them right now. And they would definitely *not* react well if I cried to them and told them all the details of my sordid love affair. And how it ended.

I refuse to stay in this house. I'm sure as hell not going to be here when he gets back.

What kind of excuse is that, anyway? *I can't do this to you.*

Give me a break.

Okay, I get *some* of his reasoning. He's damaged. He's been through a lot and he doesn't want me to have to deal with all his baggage. *But I want to deal with his baggage.* I don't *mind* his baggage. I can see *through* all that to the person he is *underneath* the baggage. I could *help* him find his way through it, if he'd only let me.

It also doesn't hurt that all that baggage comes with such … outstanding packaging. *His body,* holy hell. His *mouth* … *and what he can do with it.*

The way he held me. The way he looked at me. As he was spilling himself inside me …

The whole thing is making me want to scream and cry and do something reckless. Because I want to do it all over again. I miss him. I miss everything about him and the way he made me feel.

Damn you, Caleb McCabe.

I still have a blanket wrapped around me, and nothing else on. There are extra clothes in my car, I can only hope.

So I let myself out. I find a pair of jeans and a top in a bag on the back seat.

The very last place I want to go is back to the dorm and that empty room.

I decide to go for a drive. I crank up the music and head southeast. I have no idea where I'm going and I don't really care. I feel like putting some distance between me and the beast who took my virginity—thank God I'm rid of it is all I can say—then basically broke my heart. He's heading to Chicago to see his damn brother? Fine, I'll head in the opposite direction. Maybe I'll drive all the way to New Orleans. I've always wanted to go there. I can skip a class or two if I feel like it. I've already done the assignments.

Maybe I'll just disappear for a while. Have some fun. Hell, if Caleb McCabe doesn't want me, maybe I'll find someone else who does.

But no one else would have those soulful, violet-blue eyes. The kind that, when he looks at you, make you feel like no one else in the world even exists. That thick hair. That perceptive contemplation. Like all the thoughts he's having are somehow in tune with your own.

Or all those big, crazy-buff muscles. That hold you down while he does things to you that'll blow your freaking mind.

God.

Or that huge cock, rearing inside me, filling me with his spooling heat.

He felt so damn good.

I keep driving for a while, and the road is blurred from my tears, which I wipe away angrily. I don't want to cry anymore.

The music is loud. I start to feel tired. I guess it's not surprising, since I hardly slept at all.

Glancing down at the dashboard, I notice I'm speeding.

I realize a split second too late that I'm going *way* too fast to take the curve I'm heading toward.

I slam on the brakes as I turn the wheel.

From there, it all happens very quickly. The car veers off the road and it starts to flip in a surreal whirl and all I have time to think about is … *I wish I could've kissed you one more time.*

12

CALEB

It's after one o'clock in the afternoon by the time I get back to the house. My decision is made and now that it's locked into place, I can't get back to her fast enough.

It's been more than a day since I left Violet, wrapped only in a blanket.

My regrets almost crush me. My reasoning in that moment rages in my brain but I fight it back. I know why I made that decision. To try to save her … from myself.

But I can't stay away.

I have to have her.

My … whatever this is … lust, or something much more savage and life-changing, has sunk its teeth into me ruthlessly. If I don't find that girl soon, I feel like I might lose my grip.

I try not to go there but the thoughts pummel through my brain.

What if she consoled herself with … someone else?

Like Hayes?

I'll fucking kill him.

She's mine.

I pull into the driveway. Of course I notice that all the cars are gone. Including hers. I vaguely remember from that first day we almost met, when I saw her out the window, that she drives an older model Toyota.

Not anymore. I'll buy her whatever she wants. A Shelby. A Porsche. A goddamn limousine.

I grasp at straws. Maybe it's possible she's still here. She might have decided to hang out with Millie and Bo for the weekend. Maybe …

There's no reason for her to be here if her car isn't.

I search the house. I go down to the boat to see if maybe she went back to it. I find her dress. The shreds of her bikini. But no Violet.

Searching the main house, I bang on Bo's door.

He mumbles something, then a few seconds later opens the door. He has a towel around his waist and, behind him, Millie is in his bed, covered mostly with a sheet.

"Hey, man," says Bo. "Where'd you go?"

"Chicago. Where's Violet?"

"Chicago?"

"Where's Violet?"

"I haven't heard from her, Caleb," says Millie. "She's probably back at the dorm."

"I need the address. And her phone number."

Bo is staring at me and has probably figured out that something is going on between me and Violet. I don't have time to explain it. I don't give a damn about anything right now except finding her.

"I'll call her." Millie picks her phone up from Bo's bedside table. She calls Violet and I can hear the sound of Violet's phone ringing. "Her phone went straight to voice-mail. That's weird. She usually picks up."

Something's wrong. I don't know if it's a sixth sense or an instinct that gets honed by combat and regularly watching people close to you get shot or blown up or killed, but I can feel it. My heart and my head are both crackling with fear. For my girl. *Something has happened to her.* "Millie, I need the key to your room."

She gives me Violet's number and the key and I can't get out of there fast enough.

"Caleb?" Bo calls after me but I'm already out the door. It's a miracle I don't either die or get arrested on my way to campus. I storm into the dorm and a bunch of people are staring at me as I unlock Violet's door. But when I finally get the door open, her room is empty.

I'm standing in her room wondering what the hell to do next when my phone rings in my pocket. Bo's number flashes on the screen, but when I answer, it's not Bo. It's Millie. She's crying.

"Caleb, I just got a call from Violet's brother. The police found her. She's been in an accident."

No.

No. No. My voice is husky and low. "Please tell me she's okay."

"They're not sure yet." Millie's crying harder now, and Bo takes the phone from her. "They're still not sure how serious her injuries are."

No. No. *Not Violet.* "What hospital?"

"Memorial."

I can't even remember getting to the hospital. Millie and Bo are just arriving.

"We're here to see Violet Jameson," says Millie to the receptionist.

Please let her be okay. I'll do anything. I'll spend every waking moment giving her everything she needs. I'll open up to her and *let her in.* I'll fight my demons because if I can do that, there's a possibility I can make a future with the girl of my dreams.

If she lives.

She has to.

Because all this is my fault.

I walked out on her. I upset her. She might have been distracted by … *how sore she was. Or how pissed off.*

No wonder she wasn't in her right mind. No wonder she'd had a hard time keeping her eyes on the road.

If anything happens to that sweet girl, it'll be on me.

Again.

I won't survive this. I won't be able to handle it if anything has happened to her.

Millie and Bo go into her room and I hesitate at the door, bracing myself for what I'm about to find.

I walk in, and she's sitting in the bed. She's whole, and awake, and very much alive.

And just like that, I have a reason to live.

Her bed is facing the window. She's talking on the phone. "Mom, I'm *fine*. The doctors said I have a mild concussion, some bruises that aren't even that bad and one broken finger. That's it. There's no need for you to fly out here. They said they want to watch me overnight and get a few more test results back, then I'll be discharged tomorrow morning." A pause. "Yes. They said I was lucky to walk away from it practically without a scratch, but I guess someone upstairs doesn't think my time is quite up yet."

I'm tempted to get down on my knees and *pray* to that someone upstairs, to thank them for sparing her. It's not like them to *spare* anyone I care about, not my parents or three of my men, including my best friend, so I feel wildly grateful.

Even so, the sight of Violet hooked up to those machines does something to me. It breaks my heart wide open.

And it begins to fucking cure me. The quagmire of my psyche becomes less complicated.

This. Her. She's what I want.

Even lying in a hospital bed, she looks stunning. Her hair is vibrantly colorful in the sterile room. The playful sprinkling of freckles across her nose is too festive and cute for the scene and it just makes me fall even harder.

She sees me, and she pauses her conversation. She doesn't look all that *pleased* to see me, it's true. But I can hardly blame her for that. She's glaring at me, so I just stand against the wall with my hands shoved into my pockets and wait until I can talk to her. Alone.

"Tell Henry he is *not* to come out here," she's saying into her phone. "I'll come home for Thanksgiving and I'll see everyone then, okay?" Another pause. "How's Earl?" She smiles. "That's good. Mom, I'll call you back a little later. I've got visitors. Love you too. Tell dad not to worry. I promise you I feel fine. Okay. Bye."

She can scowl at me all she wants. I deserve it. And I've already made up my mind. I pull a chair close to her bed and I sit.

"Hey, sweetheart," I say softly.

Bo does a double-take at my endearment, but I honestly don't give a fuck. If he hasn't figured out the extent of what's happening here, he will soon enough. He's almost smiling. "Don't worry, I get it." His glances at Millie. Yeah. I guess he does.

"We'll give you two a minute," says Millie, watching me, like she's reading my angst and understanding that I really just need some space here to get a few things off my chest. "We'll get some coffee. We'll be back in ten." She gives Violet a careful hug, then Millie and Bo leave. I'm grateful. I'm about to gush and it's not something I usually do.

Just Violet. My girl. She's the only one who needs to hear what I have to say.

We're alone now and she's still staring at me. She looks pale and it's that detail that slays me. I can handle her anger but not her illness, especially when it's my fault she's here in the first place. So I just start talking and it all comes tumbling out in a big rush.

"Violet. I'm sorry. I know I'm to blame for everything. I shouldn't have left like that. What happened between you and me … well, it was the best night of my entire life and I honestly didn't know how to react to you. I thought I might have hurt you and I'm sorry for that too. I couldn't deal with the fact that I *might* have. I had no idea it was your first time and if I'd *known* that, I would have been more careful. Which I should have been anyway. It's been a long time since I've been with anyone and I sort of … lost myself. Because you're so insanely beautiful and you felt so damn good. You basically blew my head off and broke my heart in one fell swoop and it was kind of intense. And then when I had that … episode, I knew it was very likely that I'd hurt you again, even if it was more of an emotional pain than a physical one—or both, since I just don't know myself anymore and I can't be sure. Which isn't a good feeling. I've got a lot of shit I need to deal with and the memories some-times take me down into a black hole that consumes me. I didn't want to drag you down with me and I knew I would. I wanted to spare you all that. So I tried to walk away from you. But I can't do it. I *can't* stay away from you. Because I want to be the one who takes care of you and makes you laugh. I want to protect you in every way I'm capable of. I'm going to do whatever it takes to make it up to you. And to get you to trust me. And to try to make myself sane again so I don't cast shadows onto your life. I want to try like I've never wanted anything. All I really care about is being with you. I'm asking you to forgive me. If you can. And if you can't, I understand. But it won't stop me from trying even harder to prove to you that I'm sorry about what happened. I want to do more than make it up to you. I want to be there for you and take care of you. I know all this is intense to hear right now, but the other night changed something in me. It felt important. I don't know where any of this will lead, but I want to find out. I want to try to be good enough for you. I want to be honest with you. I want to heal you. And once you're feeling better, we can go out on the boat again, if you'll come with me. I'll treat you right this time. I'll be careful. We can talk about all the things you want to talk about. And I won't leave you."

She's watching me very intently. I think I detect a slight softening of her hostility, but I can't be sure.

"I'll take such good care of you," I say.

She doesn't reply. Her green eyes look barely bloodshot and it's fucking hard to handle, that she might still be ill or upset. *My fault.*

"Will you at least think about it?" I don't think all the stuff I've said this entire year would add up to what I've just gushed to Violet.

Oh, fuck. She's crying. A tear paints a shiny line down her pale, flawless cheek. *Now* what have I said to hurt her?

"Nothing was your fault except leaving me," she says quietly. "I don't forgive you for leaving me."

She's talking to me. It's a good start. "That's okay. I don't blame you."

She's quiet for a minute. Then she takes my hand and starts weaving her fingers through mine and she says, "But I'm glad you came back."

13

Violet

WHEN I WAKE UP, I try to remember what happened, but it's hazy. I lost control of the car. I took a turn at speed and realized I was about to crash. After that, everything went black. And I woke up here. In this hospital room, hooked up to an I.V. drip.

The doctors said it was a miracle that I wasn't hurt worse than I am. Or even killed.

I feel woozy from the painkillers. I have a bruise on my shoulder, a minor concussion and my left hand has a brace on it for my broken pinky. Other than that, I feel fine. I was wearing my seatbelt and the airbags deployed. My car is totaled, but I'm relieved to have walked away as unscathed as I am.

Apparently the people driving behind me saw my car veer

off the road and called an ambulance. Of course, once my family heard, they all threatened to jump on the next plane. But I don't want them to. All I really want to do is go back to my quiet dorm room and sleep. Then I'll immerse myself in my studies and football games and whatever else it takes to … forget about a certain moody hunk who I'm still furious at.

I've decided I really *do* want to go to New Orleans. But not yet. I want to go to have fun, not to escape.

And I don't need *him* to have fun. I'll … find someone else. Someone even hotter.

There's not a man alive who's hotter than Caleb McCabe.

Someone a lot less surly and fucked up. *That* part would be easy.

But would he look at you the way Caleb did that night, when he connected with you on some crazy level that wasn't just physical but … something a lot more than that? And don't even get me started on the "physical" part of it. Good luck finding anyone who's that good-looking or can hand out orgasms at the drop of a hat. If it was that outrageously good your first time, when it's supposed to be painful and daunting and awkward, imagine what else *he can do. And then there's that outstanding detail of how freaking* big—

I wish I could tell the little voice inside my head to shut up.

My mom calls again and I talk to her for a while. While I'm talking, Millie appears at the door, with Bo, and I'm glad to see them. Except the part where Bo looks a little too much like his brother today and it's just compounding everything. Millie's carrying a bag of my stuff she got from our room. She sets it on a chair.

And then—*shit*—in walks Caleb.

He's wearing a black t-shirt that shows off all his muscles. He looks tired, but annoyingly gorgeous. His military haircut is growing out and it's thick and unruly, like he's been running his hands through it. His skin is deeply tanned, from the desert, maybe, he's tall and beautiful and has that stormy, uncontrolled energy that immediately changes the entire vibe of the room. Hurricane Caleb.

The way he's looking at me is making me feel even more light-headed.

"Okay," I say to my mom. "Yes, I'll call you a little later. Okay. Bye."

I end the call and Millie gives me a hug. Bo does our little fist pump thing. "Glad you're okay, kid."

"Thanks, Bo."

They can't help noticing how intense Caleb is and they pick up that he wants to talk to me. I'm not even sure I want him here right now. I'm tired and still reeling from my near-death experience and I don't know if I can handle his intensity. Besides, he's a bastard, he's proven that. The sensible part of my brain is telling me to steer clear. To take it as a sign that this guy will just use me and ditch me because that's his style.

You don't think that's his "style," Violet.

Okay, maybe I don't. Maybe I know why he left. And

now, at least I can give him a tiny bit of credit for coming back to see if I'm okay. Maybe.

He pulls a chair up next to my bed and says, "Hey, sweetheart."

Sweetheart.

A part of me might have already forgiven him. He looks so sad. It's pretty obvious he's swimming in regret and I find myself thinking that I hope he doesn't regret … *all* of it.

Millie and Bo leave to get some coffee and to give us a minute.

Caleb takes a deep breath. Then he starts talking. *Really* talking. And the things he says to me are so heartfelt and so beautiful that, as he's talking, I basically fall in love with him. Again. Or even more. He's sorry. He thought he hurt me. He doesn't want to drag me down with his issues. But he can't stay away. He wants to give me everything. He wants to take care of me and protect me and be with me.

And I want to let him.

It's good that he can let it all out like this. It gives me hope. If he can do that, then there's a chance that he can start to heal. That some of his trauma will get easier in time.

"So … what do you say, Violet?" he says. "Will you at least think about it?"

I guess I could think about it.

You already have.

I never really liked that dorm room. His lake house sure is a lot nicer.

And he'll be in it. Taking care of you.

I don't want to let him off the hook *too* easily. I tell him I'm still mad at him for leaving. Then I tell him I'm glad he came back. He looks so relieved and sad and grateful and gorgeous, I reach for his hand.

He sits next to me on the bed.

"As much as I'd like to blame my temper tantrum and my speeding around a hairpin curve on you, I won't," I tell him. "Those things weren't your fault. The only thing you did to hurt me was walking away."

"That's not going to happen again."

I could hold a grudge and make him prove himself. But, to me, he already has. Besides, when you total your car and walk away with barely a scratch, it makes you appreciate being alive. And it makes you want to make the most of every minute. "In that case ... yes."

"Yes?" He's so relieved about this, it breaks my heart just a little bit more.

"The doctor said I can be discharged tomorrow."

"I'll bring you home with me. Then I can make sure you're recuperating properly."

Like Caleb said, we can't know where this will lead. But, also like him, I want to find out. "Where'd you go?"

"To Chicago. To see my brother. He helped me clarify a few things."

I almost ask him what things he's talking about, but I think I already know. "You *did* treat me right when we were out on the boat, by the way."

His expression has a lot going on. What is it about Caleb McCabe that draws me so completely *in*? Some heady cocktail of complexity that meshes with my own, mixed with a whole lot of A-list alpha. The combination really is devastating me. Even with all his baggage—or maybe partly because of it—he's basically to die for. Like the song lyrics go, wild mustangs couldn't drag me away from him, especially now that he's bared his soul to me and has confessed that he's *mine*.

"I'll only come home with you if you promise me something," I tell him.

"Name it."

"Don't walk out on me again."

"I told you. There was a reason for that. And it won't happen again."

"There will be hard times, Caleb. You'll have more nightmares."

"I know."

"It helps to talk. To me, and to other people."

"I know. I'll try. I will."

He's still holding my hand. "I really am glad you came back."

Caleb gives me a look that's caring and soulful … and more than that. There's an edge to it. A *hot* edge. Like he's thinking about some of the things *I'm* thinking of … *of the way he gripped me as we looked into each other's eyes and came together.*

And how I want him to do that again.

By the time the doctors get the paperwork signed for my release, it's mid-afternoon. Caleb only left last night when the nurses threatened to call security because visiting time was over, but he's back as soon as they'll let him in.

He's showered and he's wearing worn jeans and a navy blue polo shirt. He still wears his dog tags and I can see the chain at his tanned, corded neck. Both the nurses in the room turn to stare at him when he enters the room. One of them gives me a *damn, girl!* look.

He keeps his arm around me as we walk to the reception desk, then as soon as I've signed out, he carefully lifts me into his arms.

"Caleb, I can walk."

"No."

"I'm not one of your soldiers that you can order around, you know." He's being controlling as hell, even if it is kind of sweet.

"It's more of a safety precaution than an order. You might still be dizzy from your concussion." Before I can even point out that the doctor said my concussion was very mild and that a couple of Tylenol should do the trick, Caleb carries me out to a behemoth of a black SUV. It's shiny and looks brand new.

"Is this a Hummer?"

"Yes. I bought it this morning. You clearly need something fortified."

I stare at him for a second. "You bought it—?"

"To drive you around in." He lifts me into the passenger seat and leans over me to do up my seatbelt. "How's your finger?"

"Fine."

"And your shoulder?"

"Also fine."

He walks around the colossal vehicle and climbs into the driver seat.

"I can't believe you went out and bought a Hummer this morning. Who does that?"

He grins at me and pulls out of the parking lot. "Me, I guess. I'm as surprised as you are, but I won't risk any more injuries."

We drive through town and eventually through his gate and up the curved driveway to his lake house. "Stay right there," he says. He gets out and strides around to the passenger side before opening the door and lifting me out.

"Caleb, you really don't—"

"Let me." Caleb starts carrying me into the house and up the stairs. He's so freaking *muscular* he doesn't even seem to register my weight at all.

"What's your rank?" I ask him.

"Corporal. Why?"

"Are you sure you're not a general? You act like one."

He laughs and carries me into a bedroom, which has a wall of windows and a killer view out over the lake. I can see all the way down to the boat, still moored there by the dock where we left it. *After a night of blistering passion that changed us both and bonded us in a way that can only be described as profound.*

"Caleb. It's four o'clock in the afternoon. I don't need to go to bed."

"You need rest. Don't worry, I'll stay with you. I'm not going anywhere." I don't know if I've ever met a person who's so *sincere* all the time. It's kind of adorable.

It's also exasperating.

He sets me onto the plush, gargantuan California king.

"Caleb?"

"Yeah?"

I sometimes wish I wasn't the kind of person who blurts out the first thing on my mind. "Is this the master bedroom?" The door into the master bathroom is open and I can see marble walls and a bath so big it looks like a jacuzzi.

"Of course." Like he's offended by the thought I might be placed anywhere else.

I do manage to hold my next question. *Where are you sleeping? With me?*

I guess we'll figure that out as we go, like all the other things we need to figure out.

"I'm going to make you some food. You need to keep your strength up."

He gets me settled in the enormous bed.

"The remote to the T.V. is here, on the bedside table." I notice then a wall-mounted flat screen that's almost as big as the entire wall. "I'm going down to the kitchen. I'll be back in ten. Will you be okay?"

"Yes, Caleb."

After he leaves, I go into the bathroom. Even the bathroom has a view. There's a marble and glass walk-in shower and the huge jacuzzi. Sitting on the edge of it, there's a small jar of bubble bath. It's funny that Caleb would have bubble bath. I have a feeling it's not his. Maybe it was his mother's, from a long time ago. Either way, the whole set-up is calling my name. Those hospital sponge baths weren't particularly satisfying. I decide to run myself a bubble bath.

I've left the door open a crack. By the time Caleb returns, I'm happily ensconced neck-deep in hot, jet-infused bubble heaven, aside from my left hand. I leave it draped over the side so I don't get my brace wet.

He barely knocks as he pushes the bathroom door open, stepping inside and filling the room with his brazen, squally glory.

"I hope you don't mind," I say, as he stares at me. He's still dressed in his jeans and his polo shirt. He's barefoot. "I helped myself to your jacuzzi."

It's hard to know how to gauge our … relationship, or whatever this might be called. *We've already had sex*, is the elephant in the room. *Really good sex.* Not that I'm an expert or anything but I do know enough to realize that what happened the other night wasn't just good … *but fucking spectacular.* We've had a stellar and life-changing one night stand, broken up, had several near-death experiences, a meltdown or two, a couple of heart-to-hearts …

… and now we're here.

In this moment. Which feels like a beginning of sorts. We've both confessed that we're giving this—us—a try. But we haven't laid out the particulars of how it's all going to play out. I don't know if this sudden attachment we seem to have for each other will last. What I do know, though, is that I *want* it to. I want to stoke it and forge it. I want to be with him and help him and heal him, if he'll let me. Maybe it's too quick to feel this engaged. But it doesn't *feel* too quick. It feels, like Caleb said, *important.* It feels like I have a lot to lose.

So I say, "Do you want to … come in?"

He doesn't even hesitate.

Or take off his clothes.

He steps in and lowers himself into the bubble bath with me, fully clothed. There's so much of him, some of the bubbles and water splash out onto the floor.

"*Caleb.* What are you doing?"

"Coming in."

I laugh because he's all wet and covered in bubbles … and so damn beautiful I think I might absolutely love him. "You're splashing all the water out."

Caleb doesn't seem to care. Because he splashes a lot more water out when he leans closer.

He doesn't touch me. He just leans back against the side of the tub next to me, where one of the jets is. The water fizzes up around his neck. There are bubbles in his hair. "We'll take it as slow as you want this time," he says.

This time. As opposed to last time, when we dove right in at the deep end. "You know, most people don't take baths fully clothed."

He gives me a lazy, mock-surprised grin. This playful side of him is even more heart-breaking than the brooding one. "You don't say."

He pulls his shirt over his head, creating havoc with his hair. He balls up his soaking shirt and tosses it over the glass door of the shower. It's hard not to stare at his super-buff, bronzed, hair-dusted chest.

"Nice throw."

"Thanks. I used to be a quarterback."

I can picture it. The cool-headed tactician, who turned his focus to precision shooting. It's a similar skill, after all.

He relaxes, like the beating water at his neck feels good.

I can see the scatter of scars across his chest, where he's still healing. They seem wrong there. Caleb's body is lean and perfectly proportioned, as though sculpted by nature with particular care. These little imperfections, put there by violence, make me feel inexplicably sad. It's like witnessing the consecration of something sacred. I know now that his scars run much deeper than these wounds. And I have an overwhelming urge to do whatever I can to heal him in every way I'm capable of.

He notices the bruise on my shoulder. Very gently, like

he's having similar thoughts, he smooths his thumb over my skin. "Does it hurt?"

"No." I touch my fingers to the scar over his heart. It's one of the bigger ones. It must have come close to killing him. "Do these?"

"Not really."

I reach for his dog tags, running my thumb over the raised texture of the lettering. *MCCABE. C.J.* His blood type, *A POS.* His social security number. *USMC L. CHRISTIAN.*

I can't really bring myself to be shy or stand-offish or puritanical. *He's too freaking hot for that.* His muscles. His compassion. His sapphire eyes. *The memories of what his tongue can do.* The combination of all the dazzling details of him is kind of burning everything about me.

"Come here," he says, his voice low.

I ease myself onto him so I'm half-floating and half-lying on top of him. I'm very aware of my nakedness, the fullness of my breasts as they rub against his hair-roughened chest. His skin is the color of rosewood, and the smooth, vivid richness of absorbed sun on his skin fascinates me, like he's still radiating some of its heat and its light.

"We'll take things at your pace this time," he says.

He still thinks he's wronged me, or hurt me. He thinks he's capable of damaging me, by giving me all of himself. "We took things at my pace *last* time, Caleb. What happened on the boat was *me* just as much as it was you.

The only thing I don't want you to do is hold back from me. That's what got us into trouble last time."

His eyes are smoldering with regret, but also hope.

"I *feel* you, soldier," I whisper.

His warm hand slides under my hair, around the nape of my neck. "I feel you too, baby girl." He kisses me, fitting his mouth to mine, tasting, delving into me more insistently, feeding me with his taste and his fire.

He lifts me, being careful with my hand, and somehow at the same time he steps out of his wet jeans. He dries us and carries me to the bed, where he lays me down. His rough, desperate passion, like the night on the boat, is still there, but it's tempered with dedicated care, to making sure he's giving me exactly what I need and want.

I pull him down to me and I kiss him, touching my tongue to his perfect bottom lip, licking into his mouth.

Caleb kisses me for a long time, until my entire body is simmering with lust. He moves down my body lazily, kissing and licking my skin, painting every inch of me with raw, ripe desire. "Your *beauty*," he murmurs, "the *feel* of you and the *taste*. Fucking hell, honey. You're the most addictive thing on this earth. I'll never get enough." His mouth fixes over my nipple, drawing in strong, hungry pulls. One, then the other, sending currents of heat to my core, where I feel warm and soft and brimming.

He starts kissing a line down my stomach.

Agonizingly—and very deliberately—taking his time.

He lifts my knees and opens my legs, and settles between them. "Relax," he whispers. "You're going to like this."

Very slowly, he licks his tongue gently inside me, then all the way up, where he licks my clit in teasing little flicks. He does this again and again, pushing his tongue deeper, then laving his tongue to open me, playing my clit with his wickedly stealthy mouth.

I'm moaning his name. I'm pleading.

He eases two fingers inside me, curling them and rubbing a *very* sensitive place. At the same time, he sucks on my clit, milking the tender nub in a compounding rhythm. I lose myself completely. The tight clenches of pleasure spiral through my body in severe, nearly-unendurable surges.

Even after the ripples die down, Caleb kisses my pussy, licking me lightly. *Lovingly.* It's a crazy, stunningly intimate feeling.

He climbs up my body and teases me with his rock-hard length. I arch up against him, causing the tip of his cock to slide inside my tight, slippery body.

Caleb's head drops and he presses his face into my neck. He groans. Then he, slowly, slides himself all the way to the hilt and it makes me wonder if we're *designed* for each other because just that one, thick, perfect glide makes me start coming again. The inviting squeezes of my inner muscles so tightly around him make him growl and thrust and lose his composure and it's *this* part of him I almost love most of all: the wild, uncontrolled passion. His liquid heat floods me in spooling bursts and I know for a fact I'll never, ever get enough of this.

We make love all night. We doze, connected, then we kiss and grind against each other with gripping hands and do it all over again. We make love in positions I never even imagined. There's a desperation to it that I can't entirely explain, except that I think we both just found the love of our lives.

It's an intense, needy, exquisite feeling so we just go with it.

Until we're both completely spent.

"I think that last thing you just did might be illegal," I whisper. We're sweaty and exhausted and fully entwined.

"I won't tell if you don't," he murmurs, holding me as close as it's possible to do.

MOVEMENT WAKES ME. And an anguished groan. I can barely make out his murmured words.

He's thrashing in his sleep. His nightmare is gaining momentum.

"Caleb," I say softly.

Carefully, I touch my hand to his chest. "Caleb, it's just a dream. I'm here with you. You're home. You're safe. I'm here and I'll take care of you."

He's breathing hard, but deep down, he seems to hear me.

I kiss his face gently and croon to him. "Wake up. Everything's okay. I won't leave you."

Slowly, he starts to calm. His eyes are still closed and his chest rises and falls with his heavy gasps for air, but he's listening. I say it because I think he needs to hear it. And I say it because I want to. Because a long time ago, I never got the chance to say it when it mattered most. "I'm here and I'll keep you safe. I love you."

His eyes open. He blinks and I can see he's returning to himself, regaining consciousness and beginning the ascent out of the harrowing maze of his dreams. He turns toward me. "Violet?"

"Yes, it's me." I gently kiss his lips. "I'm here with you."

He's staring at me in the darkness like I'm a vision. Or a savior. His eyes are blue embers in the moonlit night.

And I find myself telling him the one thing about my life I never talk about. I have no idea why I would, but something about this moment feels right. "My brother Joe committed suicide when I was seven. I know what it feels like to lose someone. And to feel like it's your fault. Like you didn't do enough to save them."

I can tell that Caleb is still in limbo, half mired in the lingering effects of his nightmare. "I'm sorry," he whispers.

And I sense an opportunity here. An open window into his dreams that closes in the bright light of day. "Who's Logan?"

He goes still, and he stares into my eyes, so deeply.

It could backfire. He could shut down or react in a way that neither of us were expecting. Trauma can do that. Like that night he ended up in the lake.

Tonight is the second time I've heard him call out that name. He said the same name just before he jumped overboard.

I kiss his face again, very softly. "I'm here. I love you. Who is he?"

"My best friend," he murmurs darkly. "It was my fault."

"Tell me what happened." One of the textbooks said it's better to make gentle commands than to ask questions. I don't know if that's true or not, but it kicks in now.

He's still not fully awake, but in some midnight half-world of trust and sorrow, he gives me what I want. The crux of his pain. "I saw the movement. In that far, upper window. If I'd just done it then, he wouldn't have been shot twice. One of the bullets hit him in the head. The other in the heart. They ripped him apart. By the time we got to him, he was all over the dirt. I was picking up pieces of him and trying to put him back together. I couldn't believe it was him and not me. There was no justice in that. He was a better person than me in every way."

I have to keep going, even though I can feel the agony in him. I can hear it in his voice. I want him to release it. This is the way through. *This* is how I can start to heal him. To find the most painful things imaginable and start to open the lid so they can breathe and dissipate and pour themselves out. It's the only way to begin to make them easier to cope with. "Why didn't you fire at the window when you saw the movement?"

"I couldn't identify the target. It's the cardinal rule. Always identify the target."

"It could have been an innocent person. A woman and her a baby. A little girl or a little boy. You couldn't risk that. You did the right thing, Caleb."

"I sensed it, though. I *knew*."

"You couldn't have *really* known, though. Not really. That's why they make that rule. Just in case. It would have been worse if you'd been wrong. Logan would have understood that."

I can see the second he's fully awake. He's back with me now, and the haunted shadows begin to fade to the fringes. His voice is still husked with emotion, but steady. "I know. It's war, but it's still so sudden. And unexpected. And unbearably final."

He's doing it. He's *letting it out.* "I felt that way too, with Joe. I wished I could bring him back, so I could sit with him one more time. I had this feeling I could have talked him out of it." It's another thing I've learned, that talking about other people's damages can help a person deal with their own. Tonight, though, I'm not bringing it up because it's a method in a book. I'm talking about Joe because it might help Caleb, and it might help me. It might forge a deeper bond between us because our souls are both damaged in this irrevocable way. I don't know. Lives are not clean. Legacies are messy. Memories are personal. It helps to work through them as best you can.

"You were seven?" He wipes my tear with his thumb.

"It was four days before my eighth birthday. I was so mad at him for that. That he would ruin my birthday. And miss my party. Which never ended up happening."

"He must have been dealing with something that was bigger than him."

I've never heard it said like that before. It helps, more than anything ever has. "I guess he must have, yes. And if Logan were here, he'd be telling you that you're just as worthy of this life as he was. And that you did the right thing by making sure."

Caleb holds me close and I can feel his heartbeat. "Maybe he would."

We hold each other, all night long. For dear life, it feels like. We're holding each other as close as it's possible to be. It feels, more than anything, like we need each other.

And later, in the bright light of morning, still, that feeling clings to both of us.

Caleb seems changed by it. Almost strengthened by it. Before I'm even fully awake, he climbs on top of me, holding some of his weight so he doesn't crush me. I can feel his hot, gargantuan cock pressed between us. He kisses my lips softly. "Hey, little dream angel."

"Hi."

He seems lighter this morning, like some of his angst has been set free. "You know what you did last night?"

"What?"

"You showed up in the middle of my nightmare and led me out of it."

"I did?"

"You did." He's gazing down at me and all I can do is stare. His face is so beautiful to me, rugged and masculine with its shadow of stubble, bronzed from the sun, which highlights the blue of his intense, vivid eyes. His shock of thick dark hair is a mess. I weave my fingers through it, holding him there. I don't ever want him to move.

"I'll do it every night if you need me to."

He gives me a look that's soulful and connective, and I feel a sting behind my eyes. I always have been a crier and Caleb revs up so much emotion in me, I've practically been crying since the first second I met him.

I squirm a little and his big bulk rubs against me. I'm still wet from all the cum he spilled inside me during the night. He eases the head of his cock inside me, pushing his length all the way into me. The slow, thick slide starts to make me come just like that. It's the eighth wonder of the goddamn world, I've decided. A freaking orgasm wand.

"Move in with me." His voice has that deep, rasped edge to it that I can practically feel as he begins to work a deep, unhurried rhythm.

"Are you sure?" I gasp.

"Yes. Or I'll have to move into your dorm with you. I need you. To guard my dreams for me."

The way he says it, and the nudging glide of his huge

cock so deep inside me … it's too much. I'm overcome with pleasure and emotion and I'm crying and agreeing and coming all at the same time.

"I'll guard your dreams too," he says, staring deep into my eyes as I come around him in slow, luscious spasms. "I'll make sure they all come true."

EPILOGUE #1

Violet

Eight weeks later ...

I NEVER DID END up going back to live in the dorm. When I'm not in class or studying in the library, I'm being chauffeured around in Caleb's Hummer or on his motorcycle, which he only let me ride once my finger was healed enough for me to hold on to him tight. We spend every night together, either at the lake house or on his boat.

We hang out with Millie and Bo when we can, although last time we went to one of Bo's parties, Caleb ended up lunging at Hayes and had to be pulled off of him by Bo and a bunch of the other football players. Hayes had touched my hair and said something about the color of my eyes. In his defense, he'd only just arrived at the party and didn't realize Caleb and I were together. It took two weeks for

Hayes's black eye to fade but at least he got a lot of sympathy from the groupies.

Caleb's brother Gage found a local therapist that was recommended to him, who happens to be a veteran with PTSD himself. Caleb goes twice a week and even brought me with him once. He's able to talk more and more openly about everything that happened, and it's helping.

He still has nightmares once or twice a week. But I know how to soothe him. I hold him and kiss him and whisper calming words to him. Love words. He said he can find his way back to me now, and even looks for me when the dreams turn to nightmares. He says he knows I'll be there, waiting to guide him back to the light.

We've talked about it, and I'm hoping Caleb decides to retire from active duty. I don't want to push him into anything he doesn't want to do, but he's leaning in that direction, even without my gentle but zealous encouragement. My hope is that he won't have to leave me. I know he has reasons for serving, and I admire everyone who chooses to do it, but I think he's done enough. Maybe I'm just being selfish. I want to keep him.

He once told me he was financially independent by the time he was eighteen, and he's now almost twenty-five. When I asked him about it, and what he might do if he wasn't in the Marines, he told me his investments had tripled while he was overseas.

Which basically means he has more money than anyone I've ever met.

In other words, he doesn't *have* to work. At all. Ever again. Which sort of boggles my mind. We've been talking about what he might do, aside from watching his investments grow and adding to his portfolio. He's considering starting a business, but for now, he can concentrate on taking care of me, he said, and getting well again.

I love his lake house, and he's asked me to redecorate some of the rooms if I want to, to make it ours instead of just his. I don't read too much into this, and I try to take each day as it comes. But I already know in my heart he's the one. I think I knew, if I'm being honest, that day he walked into the pool area and didn't say a word to us. We've laughed about it, how crazy that is, to feel in the electricity of a chance encounter the path toward the rest of your life.

The psyche works in mysterious ways, I know that only too well. In one of my classes, which is about relationships and how and why people either click or they don't, I've learned that some of it has to do with pheromones, some of it has to do with personality, and some of it has to do with how you relate to your past and the things that have happened to you.

I'm not sure which one of the three is our strongest bond. Each one of them feels like an ironclad alignment, weirdly. That, and the small detail that we're so hot for each other we literally can't keep our hands off each other.

Like now.

I'm packing my bag for the weekend. I'm bringing Caleb home to North Carolina with me, to meet my family.

I invited Millie and Bo too, but Bo has a football game, so they'll have their Thanksgiving dinner with some of the other football players.

Caleb comes up behind me and starts lifting the hem of my dress, running his warm, strong hands higher up my thighs.

"Our flight's in two hours," I scold him. "And we need to check in."

"I'll be quick," he murmurs. "Lean over."

His grip is ridiculous. He's been working out and exercising a lot, since he sleeps better when he does. The endorphin rushes also help.

I bend over the bed and he lifts my dress and rips my panties off.

"*Caleb.*" We've talked about his habit of destroying all my panties, but he ignores this and widens my stance.

"You're a goddess," he murmurs against my skin. He leans in, licking me in slow laves, flicking his tongue against my clit. He forces my legs further apart, pushing his tongue deeper, licking me everywhere. I arch my back and offer myself fully to him in a way I know drives him crazy. His mouth is so greedy I almost come, but then he's moving, climbing over me. I can hear him unbuckling his belt buckle and unzipping his jeans. I love the feel of his engorged, silky cock as it slides against my slippery flesh, finding entry, working the pleasure higher as he buries himself over and over.

I cry out as he takes me. His cock forces rising,

mind-blowing pleasure deep inside my body as he drives into the wet constriction of my body. He slides his fingers over my clit as he thrusts again and that's all it takes. The slick friction overflows into pleasure surges that crest and break in rippling bursts, squeezing tightly around him. He thrusts deep and holds, and I can feel the hot throbbing gushes inside me as he comes.

We're breathing hard, our bodies still locked in hot, wet pleasure.

"*Damn*, baby. Each time with you only gets better. You're killing me." He slides out of me, releasing the warm rush of his seed. "But we're going to miss our flight if we don't get going. Wait right there."

I curl up on the bed for a second to recalibrate from the tidal wave of bliss as he goes to the bathroom and wets a washcloth. He washes me. "You ready?" He lifts me and holds me.

"I love you," I tell him. My love for him feels like it's too big for my heart. I need to tell him, to release a little of it, so it doesn't suffocate me. My family always said those words a lot. We all needed to hear them.

Caleb sits on the bed and sets me on his lap. He holds me in his arms and he stares into my eyes with a note of raw, stunning tenderness. He tucks a strand of my hair behind my ear. "I love you, Violet. More than I can bear."

It's the first time he's said it to me. I didn't push him, and I didn't doubt him. I *know* he loves me. I can feel it in the way he touches me and makes love to me. I can see it in the blue burn of his eyes.

He had trouble saying the words, maybe because he's lost so many people. Maybe because he'd said the words before and he didn't want them to feel like a curse, because he couldn't save them, despite his love.

Either way, his confession only feels beautiful to me. My eyes are wet because this connection we have is so insanely sublime. I love it. I love him.

He kisses me, but then we hear a car horn honking down by the gate.

"Shit," he says. "That's our ride."

We quickly get our stuff together and Caleb messages our driver and tells him to wait for us. He carries our bags as we run down to the gate.

My family, of course, *loves* him. My brothers talk football with him and ask a few questions about the equipment he used in Afghanistan, mainly, since they know about things like rifles and tanks and so on. I try to steer the conversation back to football. Since there's a game on, it works.

Earl follows Caleb everywhere he goes, trotting behind him, slobbering lovingly. Caleb doesn't seem to mind. In fact, he seems calm when he's patting Earl and stroking his wrinkled head. Earl always did have a sixth sense for wounded souls, and a way of offering his earnest, undying support when you needed it most. Dogs are good like that. Which gives me an idea.

We take long walks along the beach with Earl and we let

him chase seagulls while Caleb and I end up having sex in the dunes a couple of times, only because my parents insisted we sleep in separate rooms, even though they know I've basically moved in with Caleb back in Michigan.

We promise to spend Christmas with my family, and my mother cries when they drop us off at airport.

The next day, I get Caleb a present.

He just got home from his therapy session and I pull him by the hand into the main room, where there's a box sitting on the floor.

A snuffling sound is coming from inside it. "I got you something," I tell him.

"What is it?"

"Open it and find out."

He walks over to the box, which moves. He lifts the lid. The puppy's face pops up and he makes a little yip.

"He's a rescue so they're not sure what breed he is, but they think he's part bulldog." I took one look at that puppy and knew he was the one.

Caleb lifts the puppy up and holds him up to his face. The puppy licks him and wriggles with pure, exuberant joy. "I can't believe you got me a dog." Caleb seems over-whelmed. In a good way. I think he likes his puppy.

"He's kind of perfect, don't you think?"

"I think he's absolutely perfect." He wraps an arm around my waist and pulls me close, kissing me. "Thank you, baby." I kiss him back because he's so damn sexy. But the puppy wants attention.

"What do you want to name him?" I ask.

"You did such a good job with Earl, I think I'll let you name him."

I think about it for a few seconds. "How about Roy?"

He laughs. A real laugh. A laugh that gives me hope and basically—even if this sounds the tiniest bit melodramatic—lights up my life. "I like it." He holds the puppy close enough so it can lick his face again. "Roy likes it too."

From then on, the three of us are pretty much inseparable. Our little family of three.

And later that night, after Caleb cooks for me and we clean up the kitchen together, I notice the sun is about to set. "Come sit outside with me."

He's heading toward the stairs. "I'll be right there. I just need to get something."

A few minutes later, Caleb comes out, followed closely by Roy, and he's carrying two glasses of champagne.

"What are we celebrating?"

"Ask Roy."

I laugh. "What are we celebrating, Roy?"

"Look what's hanging around his neck."

I lean down to reach for the thin red velvet ribbon that's loosely tied around Roy's neck. I slip it over his head, and I notice something tied to it.

It's a very large, very shiny diamond ring.

As I look up at him, Caleb is getting down onto one knee.

Oh my god.

"Violet, my sweet savior and my shining sun, I'm not perfect, but I do think I'm perfect for you. I promise to be the best I can be for you, and to spend every day of my life trying like hell to make you the happiest woman in the world. I'll give you everything I have and then some. I love you, baby. I love you so much it makes me crazier than any of the other stuff, and that's saying something. Will you marry me?"

He's blurry because I'm crying again but I kiss him and he gets to his feet and lifts me, holding me in his arms. I wrap my arms around him and kiss him like there's no tomorrow. Because you never know. And when you're *this* sure you've found the person you want to spend the rest of your life with, you might as well get started as soon as possible.

When we finally come up for air, he says, "Is that a yes?"

I laugh because I never thought I could be this happy. "Yes."

EPILOGUE #2

Violet

Five years later ...

I MARRIED Caleb the summer after my freshman year of college. We said our vows down by the lake under an archway covered in white roses. All our friends and family were there and it was the most magical day of my life. During the speeches, we paid tribute to the people we'd lost. For our honeymoon, I finally got to visit New Orleans. It was fabulous. We go back there for our anniversary every year.

For a wedding present, Caleb bought me a house in North Carolina that's close to my parents and right on the beach. He said it was an investment, but we've never ended up renting it out. We go back there all the time and spend several weeks there every summer so we can see my family.

He also bought us a house in New Orleans. I told him we didn't need that many houses, but he said he'd already paid cash for it. It's on Esplanade Avenue and is huge and full of character-infused spaces that make each day we spend there feel magical and optimistic. I'm always a little bit sad when it's time for us to leave it.

Caleb also insisted on buying me a custom Lexus SUV that has one of the highest safety ratings known to humankind, apparently.

I've told him not to, but he buys gifts for me all the time. Random, outrageously thoughtful gifts that I would never in a million years have thought to ask for. He goes out of his way to try to please me in every way he can think of. Trips and jewelry and shopping sprees. Little things too, like a single flower or a special kind of coffee I like or a pretty piece of sea glass. He cooks my favorite meals. He trucked sand in from my childhood beach in North Carolina to make a sandy beach near the little cove of the lake around the bend, where we spent our first night together on his boat. It's a place we go back to all the time. There's a cute little bay there with nice trees. It's become one of our favorite places.

I finished my Bachelor's degree and am working on getting my Master's. I'm on track to start my PhD after that, and I've done two internships, both of which have already led to potential job offers once I've finished my studies.

Caleb started an investment company, and people are literally knocking on our gate to become his clients (only once, thankfully—good thing the security system is so high-tech). He's very selective. Around a quarter of the people whose investments he handles are veterans. He charges them less and most of them have become his friends. He's grown the value of the investments he's in charge of by a mind-boggling seven hundred percent since he started the company three years ago.

We've redecorated a few of the rooms in our lake house, but Caleb's parents had such a spectacular sense of style, we've kept most of the house just as they designed it.

Caleb continues to go to therapy, but only once a month now. He rarely has nightmares anymore. Occasionally I go to his sessions with him. The running joke is that his wife's therapy is more effective than his shrink's.

I think they might be right.

About a month after we got back from our honeymoon, I went with him to visit the parents of his friend Logan, who was killed in the line of duty. We sat with Logan's parents in their kitchen in New Hampshire and Caleb told them about the profound impact Logan's friendship had on his life. He told them about Logan's accomplishments and how he was the most liked and respected soldier in their battalion. I think it helped Logan's parents to hear all that, and it helped Caleb too. We put some flowers on Logan's grave and we sat there for quite a while. After that, Caleb's nightmares became less frequent, and he seemed to let some of his angst go.

Lately, we've been having conversations about babies.

For the first few years of our marriage, Caleb seemed unsure about having children. He was worried that his symptoms might somehow affect them. I talked him out of that mindset fairly quickly. *Everyone* has symptoms of something. It's the people who are aware of this, I think, that make the best parents. The ones who try. Now, Caleb is the one who's most eager to get started.

At first I wanted to wait until I've finished my studies, but Caleb keeps saying that we shouldn't wait too long. He works from home so will always be on hand, he says, so there's no need to wait. In fact I'm sort of surprised by how encouraging he is about the whole topic, so much so that he's changed my mind about waiting. And I haven't even told him yet that I made a decision yesterday.

We're on the couch watching a football game. It's a Sunday afternoon in late fall and it's raining outside. Here, in our den, with Roy curled up in front of the fire and the lamps on, it's cozy and perfect.

I'm lying under a throw blanket with my head resting on Caleb's lap. His fingers are absent-mindedly twirling a strand of my hair. I turn my head to look up at him. "Guess what?"

"What?"

""I've decided something."

"What have you decided?"

"To go off the pill."

He looks down at me, and it amazes me that I can keep falling even *deeper* in love with my husband. In moments like these, when I didn't think I could love him any more than I already do, he keeps proving me wrong. He leans down and holds my face in his warm hands and he kisses me. Our tongues dance and slide and I can feel, since I'm on his lap, that he likes what I've just told him very much. I ease my palm over the hard ridge and unzip his jeans. I slide my fist along his growing length and I break the kiss so I can take him into my mouth. I suck on him and lick my tongue over the bead of moisture at the tip.

"I'm not going to make a baby in you like *that*," he jokes, groaning.

Which makes me smile. "I'm just getting you warmed up."

He lays me back and pushes his jeans down as he lifts my skirt. I gave up wearing panties when we're alone together because he just ends up ripping them off. He licks me, but he's impatient. And fully hard. "I'm already warmed up."

He lays himself over me and pushes his thick cock inside me, feeding himself into me inch by inch, thrusting in a way that's full of lust and love and total devotion as he stares into my eyes.

"I'd die without you," he whispers.

"Don't say that." Given his parents' history, I don't want to hear him say that.

"You're my whole heart," he says.

"You're my whole heart too, Caleb."

"I love you. Much more than you could know."

"I *do* know. You show me every day how much you love me. I feel it. I feel you. I love you."

He nips on my neck playfully. "And now you're going to feel me even more as I pump my seed into that sweet little pussy and make a baby in you." He thrusts harder and I gasp because he's so *good* at this. He knows exactly how to drive me crazy with pleasure.

He thrusts hard, and deep, working a hot, sweet rhythm that tips me over the edge. The silky spasms draw on his length, pulling and inviting his release. He comes in flooding throbs, filling me with his lustrous heat.

It lasts a long time, and with our bodies still rippling in a secret bond, he kisses my face and tells me again that I'm his life, his one true love, his reason for being whole again. "*I love my wife*," he whispers.

It's an amazing feeling. To know with such certainty. I am *loved*.

And so very in love.

EPILOGUE #3

Violet

Four years later ...

I GAVE birth to twin boys the October after I went off the pill. Caleb was *very* dedicated to the task of getting me pregnant and we spent most of that winter, when we weren't working or going to classes, in bed.

We named our boys Joseph and Logan. At first it almost felt strange, the strength of those names' ties to the memories. But now, each time I say them, I feel an almost overwhelming sense of happiness. That the memories have been given such vibrant life again.

Our twins have dark hair like Caleb's and green eyes like mine. They're identical and even *I* have trouble telling them apart sometimes. Caleb put little bracelets on their wrists—

Joe's is green and Logan's is blue—just so we don't mistake one for the other.

They're full of life and laughter and I have never been so thankful. Caleb adores them and has stopped taking on new clients so he can spend most of his time with them.

Only fifteen months after the boys were born, I found out I was pregnant again, and nine months after that, we had a baby girl. We named her Adeline Grace. We call her Addie. She has red hair exactly the same color as mine and dark blue eyes like her daddy. We're so in love with her it hurts. She is an absolute joy.

We got another puppy for the boys' second birthday, a bulldog named Gus.

Twins must run in the family because Millie and Bo have a boy and twin girls. Millie and I clicked from the very first day we met and now that we're sisters, we spend a lot of time together and tell each other everything. Our kids are a little tribe and run wild around the expansive property our families share.

I finished my PhD and am now a licensed therapist in a well-respected clinic, a goal I achieved—as I'd hoped—by the age of twenty-seven. I negotiated a contract to work three days a week so I'm not away from my husband and babies too much. The job is challenging and rewarding and is a perfect fit for me.

Each day, Caleb takes the time to hug me, to kiss me, to tell me how much he needs me and loves me. And how grateful he is that I saved him.

I'm not sure if I saved him, or if we saved each other in a thousand ways.

All I know is that I'm keeping him. Always and forever.

I'm his.

And he's mine.

Thank you so much for reading My Hero. I hope you enjoyed Caleb and Violet's love story!

Reviews are like gold to authors. They help new readers find our books. If you enjoyed Caleb and Violet's story, please consider leaving a quick review or rating on Amazon.

Below I've included the first chapter of **Arrogant Player**, the third sexy, standalone book in the McCabe Brothers series. Gage is an alpha-hole who used to be a playboy … until he meets the one woman he can't have. Gage falls hard, and I had fun taking him down a notch. He definitely deserves it!

I'm also including the first chapter of **Nashville Days**, which is the first book in the Music City Lovers series, starring Caleb's hot rock star cousins!

Xoxo,
Julie Capulet

Please come join my Facebook reader group, Julie Capulet's Romantics, where I share cover reveals, insider info and we discuss all things romance!
Join group

Sign up for my newsletter to receive FREE books, plus get sneak peeks and exclusive giveaways!
Join Mailing List

Arrogant Player

Luna LaRoux has poured her heart and soul into her waterfront bar and restaurant, which has the best sunsets in Key West. The only problem is, Luna's best friend and business partner Josie is having money problems, and with twins on the way, Josie has no choice but to sell her half of the business. Actually, it's 51%.

Gage McCabe is spending the weekend in Key West when he happens to overhear an interesting conversation. Between a very pregnant majority shareholder and her stunningly beautiful—and deliciously desperate—business partner.

Gage can't resist. The bar is obviously a thriving business, and his new partner will just have to get used to *him* calling the shots … if she doesn't kill him first. It's this detail that frustrates him the most: she seems entirely immune to his charms. Unheard of. Gage is so sure of his own allure, he bets Luna his share that she'll surrender to him within a month—or the bar is hers.

Perfect. All Luna has to do is resist his drop-dead gorgeous looks, his smug charisma and his impressive … endowments, then she'll be rid of him for good. Easy, right?

Arrogant Player is a sexy standalone enemies-to-lovers romance starring a reformed alpha playboy and the one woman he can't control … or stay away from.

McCabe Brothers Series

Chapter One

Plink. I drop one of the nails I'm holding and it splashes into the turquoise water below. I lean further over the railing of the deck of my Key West seaside bar—so far, in fact, that at any minute I might lose my balance and tumble headfirst into the water. I cling to the rough wood and feel a giant splinter slide deep into the pad of my thumb. "Shit." I ignore the pain as I hold the nail in place and bang it with my hammer.

"Now *that's* a view I could get used to."

I glance behind me.

It's Kyle, our busboy. He's a competitive weightlifter. He has veiny, pumped-up muscles that look manufactured and steroid-enhanced. "When are you going to go out with me, Luna?"

"I don't date employees, I've already told you that." Around seven hundred times. It wouldn't be appropriate. Besides, he's not my type. Sure, muscles are great but not to the point of resembling an oily, spray-tanned Incredible Hulk.

"Need help?" he says.

"If it's the kind of help that means you get on with your job, then yes, that would be fabulous." I smile at him to take the edge off.

"Come on. How about one little after-work drink tonight?"

When hell freezes over, is what I'm thinking. I don't date pumped-up gym bunnies. Or prowling suits on their conference business trips. Or drunk, over-eager tourists. And *definitely* not home-town jocks. I'm … between types at the moment. For reasons I don't dwell on, especially on a beautiful day like this one.

The sunlight glints off the water in shimmery flecks, glazing everything with its magic, or at least that's how it so often feels to me here in Key West. This little island has become my haven, as though the surrounding barrier of blue water is providing a necessary forcefield. Out there, beyond the Seven Mile Bridge, somewhere among the amber waves of grain and just before you get to the purple mountain majesties, lies my past and all my regrets. Here, I can breathe. The sugar sand and lush humidity comfort me in ways I didn't even know it was possible to be comforted. "See you inside, Kyle," I say lightly, pretending to threaten him with my hammer.

"Aw." He wanders off and I resume my work, leaning a little further over the railing, holding on for dear life and desperately hoping I don't catapult myself overboard. I bang another nail into place.

"As if that's going to help," I hear another voice behind me say. I recognize the voice instantly as my best friend, the one and only Josie Farrell. My family moved into the house next to Josie's in Cedar Rapids, Iowa when we were both nine years old. I'd just arrived from New York City still in my city clothes. Josie saw me sitting on my front step, completely lost, like I'd spent so much of my childhood. Over the course of an idyllic summer, she showed me how to hand-squeeze lemonade. How to whistle with a blade of grass. How to find the best hiding places in the barn loft during our long hazy afternoons of playing hide and seek with her older brothers. How to get good height on the rope swing before you let yourself go, to get to the deepest, coolest water of the swimming hole. We've been inseparable ever since.

Her family became my family. My family is what you'd call … what's the word for it? Broken. Dysfunctional.

Blended. Or some unhappy combination of all three. My parents divorced very un-amicably (i.e. they basically loathe each other) when I was six years old. My father ran off with his knocked-up (by him) secretary, who definitely didn't want a step-daughter in tow, especially one who was the spawn of her new husband's evil ex-wife. My mother is what you might generously refer to as a social climber. I think somewhere deep down inside her gold-digging heart she genuinely loved my father. The fact that their marriage imploded made her, in a way, give up on love altogether. So she went for money instead. Luckily for her, she was—and still is—beautiful enough to get away with it. Before the ink on her divorce papers was even dry, she moved us out of the only home I'd ever known and in with husband number two, a Manhattan real estate developer. I somehow found myself mired in the world of the super-rich. A limo driver drove me to my private school each morning. We had chefs and housekeepers, an indoor pool and gym, even a helicopter pad on the roof. My mother thought she'd died and gone to heaven. Me, not so much.

I discovered I'm not cut out to be super-rich. Maybe that sounds strange since so many people seem to crave it or aspire to it, but I just don't happen to be one of them. I spent three years living someone else's warped fantasy, which to me felt more like a gilded prison. Like being forced to wear a diamond-studded suit that didn't fit.

I prefer the simple things in life. A good friend to laugh with. A late-summer field of wheat to walk through. A beach at sunset. A cold beer after a hard day's work. People sometimes call me a hippie or a free spirit. I'm not sure if I'm either of those things. I am what I am, and it's … unique, so I'm told.

In Iowa, with its rolling hills and big blue skies, I finally felt free. I could get dirty and ride a bike and play flashlight tag in the dark. I could see the stars.

And Josie was there for all of it. Her family was everything mine wasn't. Big and loud and fun and close-knit. I found out what it feels like to laugh and to feel loved. It didn't matter that it wasn't my own family loving me. Josie's family felt more like mine than my own family ever has. So when my mother's second marriage fizzled out a few years later and she decided to move to Los Angeles for husband number three, I stayed with Josie.

The next two years ended up being a time of my life when I could have used a mother, as it turned out.

No one ever tells you the hard stuff can be harder than you ever imagined. No one tells you that some of that hard stuff is going to cut you down until you know for a fact you'll never be quite the same. Or that you're going to need more courage than you ever knew you had.

Somehow, I survived those two years.

The day after we graduated from high school, we jumped into Josie's beat-up old van and headed for Florida. We couldn't get out of there fast enough. For her, it was her one chance to get out of the town she'd been born in and had never left. For me, it was a form of recovery. I needed to get out of that town like a drowning man in shark-infested waters needs a lifeboat.

We decided on Key West for no other reason except that we liked the sound of it.

And after three days of travel, as we drove through the tiny, sun-charmed, character-laden town, I knew I'd found the place I wanted to stay. Forever is a long time, but for me, something about the lazy heat that oozes out of this place answered a craving in my soul that was hard to explain. I still can't see myself ever leaving.

We got jobs as waitresses. We found a run-down one-room apartment, swam in the ocean and saved all our money. Turns out waitresses can earn good tips in Key West.

Three years later, when Josie's father died and left her a small inheritance (her mother had died years earlier, before I met her), we pooled all the savings we had, I sold an emerald bracelet Stepfather Number One had given me for my eighth birthday, and we somehow managed to scrape together enough money to put a down payment on a business that had just come up for sale. Our bar, where we'd worked all along.

It's a business that could do with a few upgrades. Okay, more than a few. It costs a lot of money to run—more than we ever anticipated, and exactly as much as it earns, barely —but I like a challenge. We jumped in at the deep end and we're trying like hell to learn how to swim. That was exactly ten months ago. "We're going to have to get this deck repaired by someone who actually knows what they're doing, Luna."

"I know. We will. But we can't afford to right now," I say cheerfully. I climb back over the railing. I'm wearing a cut-off pair of jean shorts and a fitted pink t-shirt with our bar's logo on the front. *Sea Breeze*. Which is now very dirty from my handywoman failure. The railing doesn't look any sturdier than it did five minutes ago. "Maybe a coat of paint will help."

Josie gives me a look. "Paint doesn't hold things together, Loon." It's the nickname she gave me a long time ago.

Josie has brown hair that's pulled back into a messy bun. Her dark eyes glint with that familiar twinkle and a slightly-exasperated expression. Her cheeks are pink with health and the kind of glow that could only mean one thing. Josie found out around six months ago that she got pregnant after a one night stand with a guy she never heard from again. The discovery was a shock, of course, and the past few months haven't been easy for her, to put it mildly. We cried together, because the whole scenario reminded us too much of the reason we left Iowa in the first place.

But once Josie got used to the idea, we decided there was no reason the two of us couldn't raise that baby right here in Key West. I promised I'd help her every step of the way. Of course I will. Besides, it won't be a bad thing for that little baby to grow up watching sunsets and playing in the sand, we figured.

"How'd your appointment go?" I ask her.

Her eyes fill with tears.

"Josie." Fearing the worst, I pull her into a hug. "What's wrong?"

"It's *twins*, Luna."

"Twins?" I pull back and hold her shoulders gently as I take in this information.

"Twin boys."

"Wow. Josie. That's …"

"Scary as fuck. I know. I don't know how to raise a baby by myself, let alone *two*. Luna, what am I going to do?"

I hug her again as she breaks down. She's done a lot of worrying over the past few months and I don't blame her. We have a budget health insurance plan that won't cover all her costs. Our bar gets plenty of customers but the rougher edges of the much-needed maintenance are really starting to show. Who am I kidding, they were always showing. It would be very easy to take this business to the next level—*if* we had a pile of cash to throw at it, which we don't. We tried to borrow more but the bank said we don't have enough equity. In fact the loan officer we spoke to was amazed we got the loan we did in the first place.

But we'll figure it out, like we always do. That's the thing about life, you *have* to figure it out. There's no other choice. "You're going to have those babies right here and we're going to take care of them together. On the beach, like we always talked about."

"That fantasy included true love and filthy rich men, Luna. Not destitute single mothers."

I don't remember the men being filthy rich in our fantasies, not mine at least, but I don't bother saying this. As for the destitute single mothers comment, I let that slide. When you're seventeen and on the road to Key West, running from your past and finally excited about what your life might become, your fantasies star hot hunks with surfboards and a sensitive side. When you're twenty-three, alone, pregnant with twins and working all hours of the day and night to keep your struggling business afloat, I guess things tend to change. Anyway, I try to look on the bright side. "Everything will work out, Josie. You'll see."

"Would you get *real* here, please, Luna? I'm knocked up with twins by a man whose last name I don't even know who's now long gone. And I spent my inheritance on a failing business that needs a complete overhaul." I guess the pregnancy hormones are really starting to kick in. Then again, when she puts it like that, it does sound sort of dire. "Did you happen to see the latest online review, Loon? It went something like this: 'The food was hearty and the cocktails were strong as hell—and thank God for that because I needed four so I could concentrate less on my concerns that the dilapidated deck was about to collapse and hurl me into the sea, which, four cocktails in, would probably have drowned me.'"

I saw the review. Someone posted it last night. "That's our only one star review," I say defensively. It's the reason I got my hammer out this morning to see if I could try to spruce things up a little. But all I've got to show for my efforts is a big-ass splinter, blood dripping from my thumb and dirt all over my clothes. And what was I even thinking, trying to improve the look of the place with a hammer and a few nails?

But I'm a salt-of-the-earth type of girl. I don't sweat the small stuff. Not that being pregnant is small, but still. We've handled bumps in the road before. Including the bumpiest one of all, which I make a point of shoving back into its hidden corner of my most difficult memories.

"We'll figure it out, Josie. We'll get through this. Everything's going to be fine."

"*Fine?* How will it be fine, Luna? And how will we get through this? You don't *get through* parenthood. It's with you forever." The comment digs deep, for both of us. Tears pool in Josie's eyes. "I'm sorry, Loon. I shouldn't have said that." She hugs me. "Now I know how you felt," she sobs. I ignore her murmur. There are certain things from my past I definitely don't want to revisit right now. Or ever.

"Come on." I put my arm around her shoulders and lead her inside, where it's cool. One of our bartenders, Rico, just arrived and is starting to set up for the lunch crowd. I give him a little wave, grab some napkins and hand them to Josie. I help her up the back staircase that takes us up to our two-bedroom apartment. "It's not all bad. At least we *have* a business. An awesome one. It's what we always wanted. In time, it'll be just perfect."

I lead her over to the couch, which is in front of the windows and bathed in sunlight.

I love our apartment, even if it is "retro," as Josie generously describes it.

It's rustic and on the small side, but the views are to die for. From up here, when the sun sinks over the water, you feel like you're flying on wings made of gold. Like, despite the underbelly of desperation that sometimes infuses your days, from up here the melting horizon is so full of promise that nothing can touch you.

But now, in the blue light of mid-morning, things *have* touched us. Again. Very real things that are going to cry a lot and require healthcare and food and round-the-clock care and supervision.

"I'm going to call Owen," Josie says. Owen is her brother who lives down the street from their family home in Iowa, which is now owned by Josie's oldest brother Marlon. Her other brother Drew lives one street over. I can already see that it's this detail—one of the reasons we hit the road all those years ago in the first place—that's calling to her now. Five years ago, we couldn't imagine staying put like that. We were different from the people we knew. We had a wanderlust that no one understood except us. And I, in particular, had a lot to work through. I needed to leave, is what it boiled down to.

I bring her a glass of water and a box of tissues and set them down on the coffee table. "I'll go help get ready for the lunch crowd. You just relax and I'll bring you up some food."

"Thanks, Luna."

"We'll figure it out, okay?"

"Sure." She smiles at me weakly and it makes me sad that she's so beautiful and that the man who slept with her and left her in the dust with his babies on the way will never even *know*. We looked for him for months. He was blond and handsome and had a cool, surfie vibe—Josie's absolute weakness. *I didn't mean to have unprotected sex with him,* she sobbed after she peed on the stick and those two unmistakable blue lines showed up. *He told me he wasn't looking for anything serious. And neither was I! We just got carried away.*

It happens.

They will have made some beautiful babies.

But even though we wandered the streets and the hotels and the bars and asked around for a tall, sandy-blond Californian named Noah, he was already gone. The only thing our online searches revealed is that there are a lot of people named Noah in California.

And I don't like the defeated edge to her voice today.

I leave her to her phone call and walk past my tiny yoga studio where I do my practice every morning at sunrise. I go into my bathroom where I start stripping off my dirty clothes. I take a quick shower and pull on a sleeveless yellow sundress. I run a towel through my hair, which is dark and cut into an angled pixie bob. It has a wave to it that has a mind of its own. Even if I try to straighten it, within around five minutes it's starting to curl again, especially in the Florida heat, so I comb it into place and leave it at that.

Then I head back downstairs to help Rico and the kitchen and waitstaff.

I don't care that our bar isn't the fanciest in town. It has *character*. It's funky and fun. Original and old school. It was a case of buying the worst business in the best location, because it was all we could (barely) afford. All the tables and chairs on the deck are colorful and festive, an effect that's enhanced by the shimmering blue water behind. We have a small beach and a dock where our customers can tie up their boats or park their jet skis. Our menu is basic American fare done well.

Maybe we could get another investor. Someone who has an interest in contributing money from afar, so Josie and I can continue to run our business without too much interference. We were only just getting going when Josie found out she was expecting. Her enthusiasm hasn't been quite the same ever since, with the morning sickness and the fear, but she'll come round again, once she has her babies and settles into a routine. We'll figure out how to grow the business *and* raise her little boys.

Everything will be fine.

Continue Reading on Amazon
Free with KU!

When he falls, he falls *hard*.

Millie Baylin just moved to a new city to start college. Introverted and studious, she plans on spending most of her time holed up in the library working on her novel and keeping to herself. But when she gets dragged along to a school football game by her fun, football-mad new roommate, the hot alpha quarterback almost drops the ball at his very first sight of her.

Bo McCabe is saving himself. A hopeless romantic at heart, he's holding out for the real thing. As soon as he lays eyes on the shy stranger with the striking gray eyes and the angel's face, he'll stop at nothing to find out if she's the one he's been waiting for.

Millie thinks Bo's insta-obsession is insanity and wants nothing to do with him. But Bo is determined. Because, somehow, Millie has already stolen his heart … and he is now utterly obsessed with winning hers.

Can Bo convince Millie he's the man of her dreams?

Hopeless Romantic is a sexy standalone novella, starring an obsessed hero and the love of his life (includes three hopelessly romantic HEA epilogues!). This book is a safe, low-angst tribute to love at first sight and insta-everything (because it happened to me.

McCabe Brothers Series

Available on Amazon
Free with KU!

It's the hottest summer on record...

Travis Tucker is the lead singer in a country-rock band whose four albums have all hit number one. Life as a superstar is good. But getting swarmed 24/7 by rabid fans is starting to lose its shine. In his heart he's a romantic. He craves something real. So he decides to buy himself a country getaway to work on his next record and clear his head.

Ruby Hayes is on a mission. Nothing can stop her from fulfilling her dream of making it as a singer and songwriter. She'll spend the summer writing songs on the grand piano in the abandoned farmhouse next door. Then she's on her way to Nashville.

When Travis finds Ruby, singing like an angel at his piano, he falls *hard*. Ruby ignites in him a wild obsession and an all-consuming lust that will make this summer the hottest on record.

But will Ruby's ambition, a jealous best friend and the

demands of Travis's high-profile life come between them? Or is this a match made in country music heaven?

Nashville Days is a sexy standalone small town rockstar romance starring a hot lead singer and the sweet, sassy songbird who steals his heart.

Music City Lovers series

Chapter One

"I want to thank ya'll for coming out tonight, Austin. You know we love you." The crowd roars.

We play our last song, our newest number one hit. I can barely hear my own voice as a hundred thousand people sing along with me. It's a crazy feeling, having *this* many souls touched by your words and so fully invested, singing their goddamn hearts out. They know every note. They've lived their lives to these lyrics. They've loved, cried and laughed to these tunes. They're filling up the night with their emotion, swaying to the slow rhythm. The lights of their phones shine like a galaxy of stars.

And when we hit that final chord, the thundering cheer of the crowd is deafening. Vaughn climbs down from his drums and the three of us stand there together on stage for a few seconds, taking it all in. The applause of a hundred thousand people is something you don't ever really get used to. The adrenaline rush is just as pure as it was the very first time.

We take a final bow and exit the stage, where a swarm of security surrounds us and ushers us through a bullet-proof corridor toward our tour bus. I can still hear them chanting my name. But we've done our encores after playing for three and a half hours. We're getting close to the end of our 48-show, 38-city tour and I'm feeling it. The highs and lows and the creeping exhaustion that sets in after giving it everything you've got for months on end. We have two final shows left, both at home in Nashville. It's been by far our biggest tour yet.

I feel lit by the crowd, the music, the whiskey and the wine, the satisfaction of pouring my heart and soul into something real. Something that touches people and connects them. Every single show has been sold out. Our record is number one. Four of our songs are in the top ten. And the momentum just keeps on building.

We get to the bus and it's crowded, with groupies and people from the band and hangers-on. Our opening act, Jackson Cole, and his entourage are here, like they always seem to be. The fame and the women are new to him. He's overdosing and finding his feet, maybe. Riding our wave, to a certain extent, but whatever.

Vaughn pours three shots. Roxie gives Kade a hug, then me. She's relieved. Turns out our little sister is a genius at managing us. This tour has been bigger than we ever imagined. Now we can play our last two home shows and finally take a much-needed break before we start another 12-show West Coast tour next month.

I collapse onto one of the plush chairs. I tip back the whiskey Vaughn hands me. One of the groupies puts her hand on my arm and leans close to me. "Travis, you were amazing tonight. You're *so* good."

Do I know her? I don't think so. She might be a new one. It all starts to blur at the edges after a while. They all start looking the same. I'm no saint but I also need to *feel* something before I'll act on the constant stream of attention and adoration I happen to get. Right now I'm not feeling much of anything.

Kade hands me a beer.

"Hell," he says, sitting in the chair next to mine and clinking his bottle against mine. "Texas always has insane crowds. I could hardly even hear us." As usual, Kade's newish girlfriend Carmen is hovering around him. Roxie's not a fan. Come to think of it, neither am I. I don't usually care much who my brothers hang out with, but this girl seems to have an effect on Kade that's messing with his head. He's more moody when she's around. Jackson joked that she's our Yoko, waiting in the wings, whispering in his ear all the time about running away together so he can work on his solo album. I don't think that's his plan. Not now, anyway. We're on too much of a roll. And I can't worry about it tonight.

Vaughn laughs and cranks up the music, chugging from the bottle of Jack he's holding. He's got a fat joint in his other hand. A groupie with a lot of piercings and a ridiculously short skirt puts a pink pill on his tongue. Another girl is unbuttoning his shirt. His black hair is unkempt and long. His eyes are bloodshot, which makes them look even more blue than usual.

Roxie pulls one of the girls away from him. "What did you give him?" She pries Vaughn's mouth open but he grins at her, sort of guiltily.

"Too late," he says.

"*Vaughn*," Roxie scolds him. "Booze and weed is one thing. You said no drugs."

"Come on, Rox, I'm celebrating. Give me one night."

"*One* night? You've had three whole *months* of nights."

"I'll go cold turkey after the tour," Vaughn tells her. "I'll take a break."

We've all heard that one before. My brother is out of control, is what it boils down to. And he's only getting worse.

Vaughn has always walked a fine line. Like our father did, until it killed him. Kade and I can easily keep up with our younger brother when it comes to the whiskey—and usually do—most of the time. The difference is, we have downtimes. We lay off when we're not touring. We clean up when we feel like it.

Cleaning up isn't something Vaughn's done in a while. I'm not sure he's even capable of it at this point. Kade and Roxie and I have talked about it. We decided to finish the tour, then we'll sit him down and talk it through with him. Get him some help or check him in somewhere if need be.

None of which is happening tonight.

We're driving all night tonight so we can get back to Nashville in the morning. There's no doubt this party will still be going when we get there.

This bus has been the hub of our non-stop bender all the way through. We all got into a groove of it for the first month or two, but after a while you find yourself getting more and more strung out from the total lack of sleep and peace and quiet. Even before we left, we were hounded like this. We have a loft warehouse we've converted into apartments, a recording studio and an office headquarters in downtown Nashville. We tried to keep the location under wraps but our fans found out about it, like they always do.

"That show was mayhem," says Vaughn. Not that he minds. Mayhem might as well be Vaughn's middle name. As if to confirm this, he blows a couple of smoke rings at me.

Tonight I'm not in the mood to fight my way through crowds of people just so I can go to bed.

What I need is some real sleep. Uninterrupted by banging and knocking and people trying to get in.

I need a quiet place to hang out for a while, I decide. A

secret getaway. An old house out in the country somewhere, far from the city and the rabid fans and the never-ending parade of groupies, where there's space and fresh air and days with nothing to do except write. I can't remember the last time I was *alone* for more than a few hours at a time.

I'll find myself someplace off the beaten track, where no one even knows I'm there. I'll sleep and daydream and clear my head. Maybe Vaughn can spend some time there too, and dry out. And Kade, without the girlfriend. All three of us. We'll work on our next record. We'll write our masterpiece, uninterrupted.

I send a message to a real estate agent I sometimes use when I buy new properties. I have three houses: an apartment in Nashville that's part of our headquarters, my own house in Franklin outside Nashville that I need to get a lot more security for because people have set up fucking camps around the peripheral fences, and a condo in L.A. None of them will be either empty or quiet. I have a lot of friends and an open-door policy for the most part, which I'm now starting to severely regret. All my houses have become magnets for hangers-on and their non-stop parties.

I'm looking for another house, I text him. *A farm, maybe, at least a half hour outside Nashville. Something remote. Very private. Surrounded by a lot of land. Maybe with a barn or something I can soundproof and convert into a studio. ASAP.*

Three girls surround me. One of them touches the top button of my shirt. I'm not in the mood to party tonight, go figure. I'm strung out. *Burned* out. I'm twenty-five years old and I already feel like I'm hanging on to the end of a fraying rope. I've been burning the candle at both ends for as long as I can remember and I suddenly feel a new urge for some goddamn solitude.

One of the girls touches my hair. Another whispers in my ear. "You're *so* hot, Travis. I love you so much."

I don't even know her name.

One of the girls weaves her fingers through mine. "We want to show you something in one of the bedrooms, Travis. *All* of us."

My phone pings with a message. It's from my real estate agent. Damn, he's fast. "Maybe later." I don't know, maybe I've become jaded. I don't want to fuck just for the hell of it, not that I ever really did. I'm not an out of control player like Vaughn and I'm not a soulful romantic like Kade. I fall somewhere in the middle. I have a good time without getting serious.

But sometimes—like right now—it occurs to me that I never quite *feel* as much as I wish I did. Never in a way that makes you want to hang on to it or get excited about it or make it last. Never in a way you'd write a goddamn song about. Which is too bad. Because I write a lot of songs. Songs about falling in love and chasing after that one and only true love because you think your heart will break if you can't spend every hour of every day with her until you die.

The truth is, I'm just guessing. Because I've never experienced anything close to that kind of intensity. Which, tonight, feels sort of … sad. All these desperate souls, looking for that one magical, elusive person they can fall in love with to the point that nothing and no one else matters.

Most of them will never find it. *I* might never find it.

Which is sort of tragic when you think about it.

Like now. Women are literally hanging off me. And I feel exactly … nothing. No spark. No interest. Just … boredom. A craving for something *real*.

I stand up and move away, as much as I can in the smoky, noisy, jam-packed space. People are getting loose.

I check the message. *I've got a new listing you might want to see. It's been sitting empty for 4 years and needs some work but it's a premium property. Beaut house. 5 bedrooms. 40 mins east of Nville, remote. Sits on 100 fenced acres with its own pond, a large barn and 3 cabins. Listed at 3.5m. It's bank-owned and available immediately.*

I follow the link and scroll through the photos.

Wow. The place is mint, but he wasn't wrong. It looks dusty and unkempt. In a good way. In a no-one-will-ever-suspect-I'm-there kind of way. I'll leave it like that. I'll become a hermit for the next few weeks and completely tune out. There are pictures of the barn too. It's huge and rustic. And the old cabins, dotted around the property.

The offer is almost too fucking good to be true.

I text him back. *Let me know where to transfer the $. I'll pay cash tonight.*

I'll move in immediately. Hell, I'll drive out there as soon as we get back.

We exchange a few more messages. He confirms that the sale has gone through. He'll have the power turned on. He'll courier the keys so they're there by the time I get to Nashville.

A strange longing settles into me that feels almost like hope. More than that. An eerie sense that something's about to happen…

Available on Amazon
Free in KU!

ALSO BY JULIE CAPULET

I Love You Series

The Obsession Begins (free)

XOXO I Love You

XOXX I Love You More

Love You The Most (free)

Sexy Standalones

Max

Cowboy

McCabe Brothers Series

Hopeless Romantic

My Hero

Arrogant Player

Music City Lovers Series

Nashville Days

Nashville Nights

Nashville Dreams

Hawthorne U Series

Lovestruck

Fun Standalone Romcom written as J. Capulet

Beautiful Savages

Paradise Series

Devil's Angel

Wild Hearts

New York Billionaires Series

Billionaire Boss

Billionaire Grump

ABOUT THE AUTHOR

Julie Capulet is an Amazon top 25 bestselling author of contemporary romance. She writes steamy love-at-first-sight romance with heart, heat and feel-good HEAs. Her stories are inspired by true love and she's married to her own real life hero. When she's not writing, she's reading, walking on the beach, drinking wine and watching rom-coms.

41631794R00114